DATE DUE

AG10'92			
MR 26 '93			
AUG 1 5 '96			
	261-2500		Printed in USA

The Highest Hit

by the same author

Sailing to Cythera:
And Other Anatole Stories

The Well-Mannered Balloon

Simple Pictures Are Best

Strangers' Bread

illustrated by Emily McCully

The Highest Hit

by

Nancy Willard

Harcourt Brace Jovanovich

New York and London

Text copyright © 1978 by Nancy Willard
Illustrations copyright © 1978 by Emily McCully
All rights reserved. No part of this publication may be reproduced or
transmitted in any form or by any means, electronic or mechanical,
including photocopy, recording, or any information storage and retrieval
system, without permission in writing from the publisher.
Printed in the United States of America

Library of Congress Cataloging in Publication Data
Willard, Nancy.
The highest hit.
SUMMARY: A young girl involves her family
and friends in her many schemes to establish an
unusual record for the Guinness Book of World
Records.
[1. Family life—Fiction]   I. McCully,
Emily Arnold.   II. Title.
PZ7.W6553Hi   [Fic]   77-88970
ISBN 0-15-234278-8

First edition
B   C   D   E   F   G   H   I   J   K

For Barbara and Rita

The
Highest Hit

One

EVERYBODY TELLS ME I COULD BE old and rich when I grow up, but I'd rather be young and famous right now. I've got a plan for doing it, too. I keep a cigar box tied to the doorknob of my bedroom, and the sign on the box says:

PROPERTY OF KATE CARPENTER SCHMIDT

PUT YOUR MONEY IN HERE

FOR THE PEOPLE WHO HAVE NO FOOD.

My dad puts in all the pennies that stick to the bottom of his pocket at the end of the day. My mom puts in a dime every time she brushes her teeth and thanks God she still has them. Trudy the babysitter can't afford to put in anything because she just bought a new set of uppers, and even though she's only twenty-five, she goes around looking like George Washington, whose uppers didn't fit him, either. My big sister Ellen told me that. She learned it in Sunday school, but not from the teacher.

When I've collected five dollars, I'll send it to UNICEF. Then I'll start saving for the Humane Society. And when I've saved five dollars for the Humane Society, I'll start saving for the Prisoners' Aid Association. After I've taken care of the prisoners, I'll begin on the Abused Children. By the time I'm twenty I'll have helped so many people that they'll nominate me for the *Guinness Book of World Records*. That's the only way I'll ever get in because all the other ways have been used up.

Once in a while, I contribute a dime.

Every Friday Mom gives Ellen and me our allowances. Fifty cents apiece. Ellen saves hers because she saves everything. She has a whole drawer of old pieces of wedding cake that she's saving to sleep on when she gets up the nerve. Because when you tuck that cake under your pillow, whoever you dream of—that's who you'll marry. I tell her why worry about who you'll marry? You're only fifteen.

I save a lot of stuff, too, buttons and baseball cards and bottle caps and old jars—everything except money. I always spend my allowance on baseball cards, of which I have about five hundred, including Hank Aaron, who is my number one. When Trudy the babysitter saw me trudging home from school with three new packs of baseball cards the day before summer vacation, she just shook her head.

"A fool and her money are soon departed," she warned me. "And keep out of my kitchen. I just waxed the floor."

"Who's coming over?"

"Nobody I know of. It's a surprise for your mom's birthday."

This year my mom's birthday came the day the new baseball cards hit the stands, which explains why I forgot all about it till that moment. Guilt and panic settled in my stomach.

"Can I help you wax the dining room floor? It could be a present from both of us."

"No, sir. I'm wore out. Go and buy her some nice lipstick at Kresge's, or some perfume."

"I don't have any money."

Trudy put the scrub bucket on the back porch and shut the door on it as if it had insulted her. Then she pushed her long red hair out of her eyes and grabbed the dust mop and shoved it savagely under the radiator in the front hall.

"Get her something that don't cost," she said.

"Like what?" I asked.

"Draw her a picture," answered Trudy. "You got more crayons around the house than you could use up in a year."

"I can't draw anything except baseball players," I whined.

"So draw her a baseball player," said Trudy.

I know Mom hates baseball. She always complains that it makes me late for supper. I knew I could do a good drawing of Babe Ruth. I've done him about a dozen times already. Maybe it's not the baseball she hates but the bubble gum. Once every couple of months she'll buy about fifty packs of cards, throw out the gum in each pack, and fill up the old fishbowl on the piano, where she keeps the rewards. I get a baseball card each time I practice my lesson, and I generally lean the card against the music so Hank Aaron or Catfish Hunter can watch over me when I'm playing and sort of encourage me.

On the other hand, she already has so many of my drawings I knew one more wouldn't make much of a present.

"I can't draw her a baseball player," I said.

"You could rob the people-who-have-no-food box," suggested Trudy.

It so happens that Trudy married a man who robbed a grocery store while they were on their honeymoon. I could have mentioned this, but I didn't.

"My dad counted all the money in that box last night. He said I should send it in right away and not hoard it."

Trudy shrugged. "Next time you better save for the Needy Children's Fund. Then when you're down and out, you can help yourself. Did you lose that front tooth yet?"

I had a tooth so loose that I could lop it right over its neighbor. My mom made a special bag out of white velvet to hold it when it comes out and to keep the money I'd get from the tooth fairy. I wiggled the tooth hopefully, but it hung on for dear life.

"You could give your mom a tooth-wiggling lesson," said Trudy. "She's a teacher. She likes lessons."

"But she doesn't have any loose teeth."

"She might have one or two," said Trudy. "She told me her gums are going bad on her, same as mine did. Crawl down and see if you can spy my barrette under this radiator."

I scrunched myself down and peered all around but didn't spot so much as a marble. And I thought about what kind of lessons I could offer Mom. Every summer she takes the drivers' training course at the junior high where she teaches American history two nights a week to grown-ups. She still doesn't have her license, but she says she's learning a lot.

"Did you find it?" asked Trudy. "It's blue plastic, and it keeps my hair real neat. My hair is my best feature," she added, smoothing it with the back of her hand.

I left her looking under the sofa and went outside to ride my bike. I thought I'd ride around the block, but I had to pass Walter's house. He was playing in his front yard because he's not supposed to leave it, even though he's nearly ten years old. I could tell from the way he kicked his old broken soccer ball around that he had nothing important to do. So I speeded up but he saw me coming and threw himself over my back fender and hung on like a tick.

"Can you come over and play, huh? Can you come over, huh?"

Seeing that he'd gotten a good grip, I pulled over and parked my bike, and we kicked the soccer ball back and forth for a while. Then his little sister Frances wandered out, clutching Walter's baseball, and she dropped the ball and gave it such a mean kick that it ran into a bush and hid.

"I'll pitch," she said.

She pitched three curve balls and I struck out, and then Walter pitched, and Frances hit the first one nearly over the house.

"I'm good," she crowed. "I'm better than you."

"No, you're not," I said.

"I've been to the World Series," she said.

"When were you ever at the World Series?" demanded Walter.

"When I was six months old," she answered.

Frances is always talking about the wonderful things she did before she was six months old because she's adopted, and even her parents don't know what she was up to before they got her. For all any of us know, she might have gone on a world cruise.

"My turn to pitch," I said.

I paid great care to my wind-up, but Walter hit the ball anyway. I know I need a lot of practice because I don't belong to a regular league. On Saturday morning the kids from Holy Cross two blocks away hang around our school playground, and they'll play anyone who happens to show up. That's the only time I ever see the Holy Cross kids, except for Philip, who lives next door to us and can't hit very well and can't run very fast. He's always boasting about his cousin Tristram. Tristram can hit, Tristram can run, Tristram can pitch. Maybe Philip really has a cousin called Tristram, but I doubt it.

When I got home, Philip's mom was standing on our front steps talking to my mom.

"He's a real delinquent," she shouted. "Really incorrigible."

I wondered what awful thing Philip had done in school. He has to go to summer school because he flunked math.

"Bishop O'Hara took his gum away from him during chapel and kept it," said Philip's mother. "The amount of bubble gum he takes from kids is simply scandalous. What can a bishop do with all those packs of gum?"

"Chew it," said my dad, knee-deep in the honeysuckle. And he snapped the pruning shears at a wayward tendril.

"He's supposed to give everything back at the end of the day," she complained, "and he doesn't."

Then she caught sight of me.

"I'll bring Nellie over tomorrow," she said. "I don't know how I'm gonna hang on much longer. She's driving me nuts."

"She looks pretty healthy for sixty," said my mother.

"She's strong as a horse," said Philip's mom. "Sunday morning she broke the knobs off the TV without even turning them."

"What!" cried my mother.

"Some Baptist minister was preaching on channel 2, and she said he jumped out of the TV and bit her."

"Who did he bite?" I hollered.

Mom shook her head at me, and I had to wait till Philip's mom disappeared through the gap in our privet hedge and crossed her own yard before she told me.

"We were talking about Nellie," said Mom. "We're taking Philip's aunt tomorrow afternoon. They've got company."

"Oh."

Suddenly a terrible thought struck me. "Do I have any batty aunts?"

"No," said Mom. "She's Philip's great-aunt. You don't have any batty great-aunts, either."

That night my dad fixed dinner. He made a big tossed salad, but he forgot to peel the cucumbers, and I was still chewing on them later when I went to bed.

When Mom sat down at the dinner table, he handed her a dozen red roses and a slim package from Ellen, who was away at camp. I'd already left the envelope from me beside her plate.

Mom opened Ellen's package first, and out dropped a pair of black gloves with a little card she'd made. Mom read the message for us all to hear.

> *Roses are red*
> *Violets are blue*
> *You can wear these gloves to church*
> *to replace the ones you lost.*

"Ellen is so thoughtful," said Mom. "I don't remember even telling her I lost my gloves in church."

Then she picked up my envelope. "I hope it's a card you made yourself," she said.

"It's not a card," I explained. "It's a present."

She opened it very carefully, just the way she'd open a present wrapped in lovely tissue that she might want to save.

A little scrap of yellow paper fluttered to the floor. Mom scooped it up and read aloud:

THIS CARD IS GOOD FOR
THREE FREE BASEBALL LESSONS.

Papa burst into a loud guffaw.

"What is this?" asked Mom.

"Free baseball lessons," I said. "For you."

"But who's giving them?"

"Me," I said.

"Oh," said Mom. Then she smiled. "That's a nice

present. If I ever need baseball lessons, I'll know where to go."

"I think there's no question but that you need them," said Papa. "You can't even hit the ball with your glasses on."

Mom shot him a terrible look. "I can't learn to play baseball," she said. "I flunked gym twice in college."

"Private lessons are different," said Papa.

"Yeah," I agreed. "Private lessons are different. Remember my violin class?"

I could tell from her face that she remembered. I was five years old, and there were ten kids in the class. We met in the basement of the Episcopal church every Tuesday afternoon. The violins ordered for us never arrived. Miss Spratt, ever resourceful, made ten fake violins out of cigar boxes with rulers taped on the ends. For six weeks I bowed my cigar box with an invisible bow. Then a boy fell out of the window and broke his arm. That encouraged the other students to drop out of the class also, but not so dramatically.

My mom laughed. I knew she was thinking of Miss Spratt, too. "Okay," she agreed. "I'll take the three lessons. But we have to practice someplace where none of my friends will see me."

"The playground," I said, "early Saturday morning. That's the best time. We'll start tomorrow."

The Highest Hit

Two

THE NEXT MORNING I WANTED to leave right away, but Mom wanted me to help her clean the house for Nellie.

"I'll vacuum the guest room," she said, "and you go around the house and take down all the pictures. You can hide them in my closet."

"Why do we have to take down all the pictures?" I asked.

"Because Nellie doesn't like pictures."

I started dismantling the front hall. First I took down all my baby pictures. Then I came to the picture of my grandpa, who died last year. You'd know at a glance he wouldn't hurt a fly.

"Mom," I called, "can I leave Grandpa on the wall?"

"No," shouted Mom.

"But *why?*"

Mom switched off the vacuum cleaner. I found her in the bathroom, soaping the mirror.

"Nellie thinks all pictures are real people, right in the room with her."

"You mean she can't tell who's real and who isn't?" I asked.

"Kate, a lot of people can't tell who's real and who isn't," said Mom. "But Nellie thinks the people in the pictures are alive. And don't wipe the soap off the mirror. You can use the one over my bureau."

"Doesn't she like mirrors, either?" I asked. I

couldn't believe I'd be allowed to leave the bathroom mirror dirty.

"No," said Mom. "And no TV when she's around, either."

By the time we'd covered the mirrors and hidden the pictures, it was nearly noon. Papa came in from weeding the vegetable garden cradling two giant zucchinis.

"How's the baseball practice going?" he asked.

"We didn't have time for a lesson today," said Mom. "Nellie's coming in half an hour."

"I'll watch Nellie," said Papa. "I wouldn't want you to miss your first lesson. After all, they're free."

When we arrived at the playground, I saw Mom wince. "We should have gotten up earlier," she said.

"Oh, Mom, with this many kids around, nobody'll notice us," I assured her.

We found ourselves a spot by the fence, in the far corner of the field. I fished a couple of tin cans out of the trash basket. "The Seven-Up can is the pitcher's mound," I explained. "The Coca-Cola can is the batter's box." ·

"Where do I stand?"

"In the batter's box."

I was just showing Mom how to hold the bat when Olivia came by, all stooped over, concentrating on caterpillars. She had her lunchbox hanging open, so I knew she hadn't caught any yet. Her little brother David was trailing after her, chewing an old washcloth tied around his hand. Usually he carries a monster

puppet because he doesn't talk much, even to his sister, and sometimes he won't say a word unless his puppet says it for him. At least not on the playground, which is the only place I ever meet either Olivia or him.

Olivia ran her hand over the scarf she always wears to hide her newest home permanent. First she looked at Mom and then she looked at me.

"Is she your babysitter?" asked Olivia, just as if Mom couldn't speak for herself.

"Nope," I said.

I stepped onto the pitcher's mound and wiggled my loose tooth like the wad of tobacco I'll keep in my mouth when I'm a major league pitcher. Then I pitched Mom a fast one. She swung the bat feebly and watched the ball zip past. Dropping her bat she chased it, but it beat her to the pricker bush and rolled under.

"Is she your grandmother?" asked Olivia.

I didn't answer. I made my second pitch a slow one. This time Mom didn't swing at all. She just stood there, looking injured.

"Is she your sister?" asked Olivia.

"Nope," I said. "Hey, Mom, you got to keep your eye on the ball and swing."

Olivia picked a caterpillar off her shoe and dropped it into her lunchbox and slammed the lid on it.

"Is your mom gonna play with us against Holy Cross next Saturday?" asked Olivia.

I shrugged and watched the ball roll till it touched the fence. Olivia darted after it and tossed it straight to me.

"Can I be the catcher next Saturday?" she asked.

"Sure," I promised. I figured catching caterpillars had honed her reflexes and sharpened her eye. Last week she caught a hundred and fifty caterpillars, all brown. Then she caught a blue caterpillar, and he ate up the entire collection and died. He didn't even turn into a moth.

After twenty more pitches Mom was all in a sweat.

"How long do your lessons last?" she murmured, leaning on the bat.

"Till you get tired and thirsty," I told her. "Are you tired and thirsty?"

She nodded, too dry to speak.

"Do you have to go?" said Olivia.

"Yeah. Mom's tired. See you tomorrow."

"See you," said David, waving his washcloth.

Olivia waved good-bye and started for home. Before I could get my baseball stuff together, she came running back.

"Does your mom know how to make a whistle out of a cough-drop box?"

"No," said Mom. "No, I don't."

"Mine does," said Olivia. "But she's moved to Toledo," she added.

"I'm thirsty," said Mom.

We crossed the street to the diner. I lugged my equipment into a booth, and we ordered two lemonades. A man across the aisle from us ordered blueberry pie, and Mom cast a longing glance at it.

"No pie," I reminded her. "You're in training."

The minute I set foot in the front yard, I knew

Nellie had arrived. I heard Papa showing someone his tomato plants in the back yard, and through the trees I saw the two of them petting the tomatoes, so green and small you'd never think they're going to amount to much. And every year the miracle happens. Bushels of tomatoes. From far off, Nellie doesn't look sixty years old. She's thin and moves as quick as I do and has a white fluffy wig that makes her whole head look like a dandelion going to seed. Philip says ten men sewed together the skins of twenty purebred poodles to make it, and it cost a whole lot of money.

"How's Mom doing?" Papa called.

"Pretty good," I lied. "She hit two out of twenty."

"Not bad for a beginner," he observed.

"Mmmmmm, mmmmmm. Yes, I do," said Nellie, but not to any of us. We eyed her uneasily.

Papa looked at Mom. "You got a call from a Mrs. Revel. She's picking you up at three and taking you to church."

Mom turned deathly white. "I promised to pour coffee at the Senior Citizens' party! I completely forgot!"

Suddenly Papa shoved a fistful of money into her hand. "You have two hours. Go and buy yourself a new dress. And don't buy anything on sale."

Mom always buys dresses on sale. And they're either too small or too big, or there's a big rip in the back, or somebody has spilled ink on the sleeve. And Mom says, "I got it for a dollar, and I can fix it." And Papa says, "All you ever do is stick on some ruffles. You always wind up looking like a turkey."

I wondered if she'd buy a new one this time. I didn't mind keeping an eye on Nellie for so worthy a cause.

" 'The Flintstones' are on," I suggested. "Do you want to watch, Nellie?"

I saw Papa shaking his head at me, and his mouth shaped the words "No TV." Then I remembered how Nellie tore the knobs off the TV next door. So I said before she could answer, "I'll read to you. I know a real good book."

Everybody lay down for a nap except me. Nellie stretched out on the back porch sofa while I read to her from the *Guinness Book of World Records*. I love that book. I get up two hours before breakfast just to read it, and I've marked the best records with colored ribbons, like the Bible in church.

"Nellie," I said, "do you want to hear about the heaviest man?"

"Mmm," said Nellie.

"He was Robert Earl Hughes of Monticello, Illinois. His greatest record weight was 1,069 pounds, his claimed waist was 122 inches, his chest 124 inches, and his upper arm 40 inches. His coffin was as large as a piano case and had to be lowered by a crane."

"What did he die of?" asked Nellie. "A virus?"

I re-read the account of Robert Hughes more carefully.

"U-r-e-m-i-a. It says 'uremia.' "

A warm breeze blew over our shy, respectful silence. I didn't ask what "uremia" meant, though I was hoping she'd tell me.

"Mmmm," she said at last. "My second husband's sister died of a virus."

I began to fear the heaviest man was too depressing a subject for her.

"Nellie, do you want to hear about the official record for opening oysters?"

"All my family died of viruses," said Nellie.

"The official record is one hundred oysters in three minutes and one second by Douglas Brown in New Zealand, in 1974."

"That man behind you—tell him to go away," said Nellie.

I spun around quickly. Nobody there. But just in case she had better eyes than mine, I said, "Please go away."

Then I read to her about the largest omelette, which weighed 1,243 pounds and used 5,600 eggs. Nellie closed her eyes, and I soothed her with Trudy's story about the man who grew turnips in the shape of Teddy Roosevelt's head.

Suddenly Nellie opened her eyes and shouted, "The way these people from New York follow me around, it's enough to drive me crazy."

She jumped up and ran out the back door and across the yard so fast I couldn't catch her.

"Papa!" I shouted.

He ran out and met her at the edge of the yard, where he took her arm as if he'd been waiting impatiently all day to walk with her among his cucumbers and roses. Then I heard somebody pounding on the front door, and through the screen I saw Philip dancing up and down on the front steps. Beside him stood the biggest kid I ever saw, the opposite of Philip in every way. Philip is short and skinny and so blond that from a distance he looks bald. The big kid was tall and heavy and had lank dark hair, parted in the middle and sleeked against his ears. I thought of muskrats and other gnawing animals that I do not like.

"This is my cousin Tristram," said Philip. And he smirked.

"Oh," I said.

"He's staying till Sunday. He's an incorrigible delinquent. He killed a guy with a curve ball once."

"What a shame we can't play ball this Saturday," I said.

"Why?" demanded Tristram loudly.

I disliked him at once. "Because the junior high kids are having their regular game this Saturday, and they use our field." I hoped this would turn out to be true.

"What time do they play?" asked Tristram.

"One o'clock."

"We'll play in the morning," he announced.

"No, we won't," I said. "They practice in the morning."

Philip's face fell. But Tristram, whose lean smile seemed engraved on his face for all time, said craftily, "We'll use the Holy Cross playground. We'll meet by the church."

"Yippee," shrieked Philip. "And the team that loses has to trash Bishop O'Hara's marigolds."

Now, I could have refused such a challenge, but

Philip has it in his power to make my life miserable if he wants to, in a thousand different ways. I didn't know Bishop O'Hara because we go to the Quaker meeting-house down the street and we don't bother about bishops. But I've had him pointed out to me on numerous occasions—a plump, pink-faced man, with a bald head and a mean squint—and once I heard Philip's father complain that the bishop had given him such a long penance he thought he'd go gray finishing it.

"Trashing a bishop's marigolds is a mortal sin," I whispered, hoping it was.

But what is a mortal sin to someone who has killed a man with a curve ball? Philip and Tristram pounded each other on the head and gave rude whoops and tore home through the gap in our privet hedge, giggling.

Then I felt my dad rest his hand on my shoulder. "How about you and Nellie and me going for a drive to Baskin-Robbins? Don't you feel like an ice cream?"

NELLIE AND PAPA ORDERED

vanilla because they don't trust all the new flavors. I always get rocky road, as I have read that this is O. J. Simpson's favorite, and I can see for myself what it did for him. When we'd crunched up the last bite of our sugar cones, Papa dropped me off at the foot of our driveway and drove Nellie back to Philip's house.

Mom was already home, setting the table.

"How was the party?" I asked.

"Terrible! I had to pour the coffee, and the spigot on the urn got stuck in the open position. Then a very ritzy lady came to play the piano, and when she lifted up the lid, the keyboard was gone. Workmen had taken it away for repairs. And I got a collect call from Ellen at camp. She says somebody stole her thirty-dollar bathing suit and could I buy her another one."

"Don't forget tomorrow afternoon," I said.

Mom stopped buttering the corn. "What's happening tomorrow afternoon?"

"Your second baseball lesson," I reminded her.

"Oh, sure," said Mom.

"Saturday is your final exam, Mother."

By the time her second lesson had rolled around, a lot of kids knew about Tristram and wanted to play in the game. Walter and Frances told their mom I'd promised to take them to the playground. Today I didn't mind. Walter has long legs and runs fast, and

Frances pitches well, and we needed all the help we could get.

When Walter and Frances and me and Mom reached the playground, Philip was standing in the middle of the field and pitching, and Tristram was hitting the ball right, left, and center. Theirs was a team of two, because all the kids were standing in a circle around them, watching.

"You set up the batter's box this time, Mom."

While Mom was grubbing around in the trash basket, a girl I didn't even know came over to me and said sarcastically, "Philip says your mom is a super player." She was wearing the Holy Cross jumper and navy socks. Even on Saturday.

"Super is not the word," I said. "My mom was so good when she went to college that the gym teacher wanted to send her to the Olympics."

The girl opened her eyes very wide.

"But she broke her leg," I went on, "sliding into home plate for her hundred and fiftieth home run of the season."

Then I caught sight of Olivia, wearing an old catcher's mitt and a huge strainer taped to her face. It didn't look much like a catcher's mask, but I let it pass.

We practiced for two hours. Walter and I pitched, Frances played outfield and shortstop, and Mom made four hits.

"Only one more lesson," she remarked as we left the field. Her face was shining with happiness. "When I was in college, I never even hit the ball once. Think I'll pass the final exam?"

The thought of my mother swinging at one of Tristram's lethal pitches filled me with such grief that I could hardly eat supper. At eight o'clock, I carried my grief right into bed with me and lay there. My stomach felt all crumpled. The clock struck nine, ten, eleven. Papa turned off the TV. Twelve. Everybody went to bed. Everybody went to sleep except me. One. Two.

Then I fell asleep, too. And I dreamed that Papa went away on a trip and left Mom and me alone. His train had barely pulled out of the station when Mom caught a mysterious virus that caused her to shrink till she stood knee-high to a clothespin. The day of this awful event, it was my turn to haul all the laundry to the laundromat in my wagon, five blocks away. Mom rode on top of the dirty sheets, as happy as a bee on a hayride. I tried to keep an eye on her, but she kept climbing into the dryers and falling into the washers, and Philip's mom was folding pillowcases on the folding table and shaking her head—things like this never happened to her, she said. Then she shouted, "Put butter on her feet so she can't run away. Put butter on her feet so she can't run away."

I woke up yelling, "Butter! Pass the butter!"

When the light from the hall flooded my room, I knew I'd dreamed the whole business. Still, I felt relieved when Mom poked her head in the door.

"What's wrong with you?"

"Mom," I said, "I had a horrible dream."

"That's funny," said Mom. "You haven't had nightmares since you were a baby."

"Mom," I said, "I'm scared."

She sat down at the foot of my bed. "Why?" she demanded. "Why are you scared?"

"I'm scared that tomorrow I'll have to trash Bishop O'Hara's marigolds."

Then in the dead of night, while even the crickets slept and only the owls listened, I told Mom the whole story.

She listened gravely. She didn't say a word, only picked at the rosebuds on the straps of her nightgown. Finally she stood up.

"Nobody is going to trash anyone's marigolds," my mother announced. "You wait and see."

Four

AT ONE O'CLOCK ON SATURDAY,
Mom and Walter and Frances and I walked the two
blocks to Holy Cross. Mom looked elegant. She had
gotten her hair done that very morning, partly for the
game, partly because Papa told her she looked like a
grasshopper and would she please cut her bangs. Now
she kept touching her new curls, as if she thought they
might drop off unless she reminded them not to. She
had put on the white sunback dress she wears whenever
she takes me shopping.

Tristram was already there, the only player on the
field, swinging his bat against invisible opponents for the
fans that lounged in the grass at the edge of his
kingdom. Even the gravestones seemed to be watching.
Through the open windows of the church, a thin ribbon
of music floated out. I wondered who was playing the
organ.

The bishop's marigolds watched, too, lined up
against the north wall just the way the bishop makes
kids line up for everything. The Lord will no doubt call
on him to line us up for the Last Judgment.

I said hi to Olivia and David and Philip and the
usual gang. But who was the little group of new kids?
Each time Tristram let the bat swing, they'd turn to
each other and their fingers drew shapes on the air,
quick as if they were knitting, and they never made a
sound.

"I didn't know Saint Jude used this place," said
Mom.

"Who's Saint Jude?" I asked.

"That's the school downtown for the deaf. See, they're using sign language."

We stared at them in open admiration.

"Can anyone learn sign language?" asked Walter. "It would be such a neat way to signal plays."

"I learned it when I was a baby in Paris before I was adopted," said Frances, "but of course I've forgotten it by this time."

"Maybe when you get to know some of the kids, they'll teach you," said Mom.

Suddenly Philip was waving his batter's hat and jumping all over us like a puppy. "Batter up! Batter up!" he hollered.

I tossed the quarter: heads, Holy Cross, tails, Grand Avenue Elementary. George Washington smiled up at us from the dust, and Tristram grabbed a bat and started pounding it to bits.

I threw the opening pitch.

To make a long story short, Tristram hit a home run.

The fans from Holy Cross cheered. Out of the corner of my eye, I saw the hands of the deaf children leaping like birds. Pretty soon somebody pushed Philip into the batter's box, and I pitched him a hard one. He hit a pop fly. Walter darted out from nowhere and caught it. I turned to wave encouragement to Mom, who was covering the outfield. She was sitting on a tombstone, her hands folded in her lap.

Now it was our turn to bat.

First me. I put on the batter's hat, and Tristram went into the wind-up, grinning like a pirate. The ball went right for me, as if it had some grudge against me. I jumped back.

Strike one.

Second pitch. I swung the bat, so as not to appear terrified.

Strike two.

On the third pitch I closed my eyes, heard a sharp crack, and made it to first.

When Frances came up, she made it to first, and I ran to second.

Olivia pushed Frances to second and me to third. The bases were loaded when Mom, adjusting her new curls, set the batter's hat on top of them. It didn't fit. It sat there like an apple waiting to be knocked off.

The first pitch would no doubt have killed her if she hadn't jumped backward. She frowned at Tristram. "You should never throw a ball that hard," she scolded him. "Never. It's not safe."

Tristram lifted his upper lip and showed his fangs, the wax ones he bought at the drugstore.

Whizz!

He pitched the second ball even harder.

Then you could see from Mom's face that she had discovered the truth. He really was an incorrigible delinquent, and he deserved to be kept after school and have his bubble gum confiscated and a lot of other bad things done to him as well.

When he pitched the third ball, Mom struck. I

heard a huge clap of thunder. The ball soared like a rocket over the trees, their silence ripped by a loud crash.

I closed my eyes.

When I opened them, the playing field was empty, as if somebody had erased the children and left the grass and trees. Mom was still standing in the batter's box, looking perplexed. Before either of us could run away, the chapel door opened, and a plump, pink-faced man in a cassock rushed toward us.

"Forty Paternosters for all of you!" he bellowed, "and fifty Hail Marys! And it'll cost a thousand dollars to fix it!"

You can't run from a bishop. He has God on his side. He puffed over to us and stretched out his hand to heaven, and I followed his jeweled finger up, up, to the big round window. Something had gnawed a great hole in the top of it.

Mom pulled off the batter's hat and dropped it on the ground. "Did I do that?" she exclaimed.

"I'll show you what you did," hissed the bishop. He edged in to cut off our escape, and clapping his hands on our shoulders, he herded us inside. My eyes were so brimming with sunlight I couldn't see anything but darkness till we turned out of the side aisle into the sanctuary. It smelled so heavy and sweet, I looked around for flowers. I saw nothing but candles flickering at the feet of a saint in a brown robe, holding a baby in his arms. Over the high altar, I saw God the Father in the window. On the day I came here with Mrs.

Fitzpatrick to pick up Philip, He was wearing a hat, all round and layered like a beehive. Now the maple leaves outside were brushing the broken space over His head.

I wondered if it was proper to pray for a miracle, and in that instant my tooth dropped out and I bit my tongue. At the taste of blood, I let out a shriek.

"Be still," cried the bishop. "This is a holy place."

"I lost my tooth," I whispered.

"Give it to me," said Mom. She held out her hand.

"I ate it. By accident."

And at the loss of that tooth I'd been banking on for months, I burst into tears. My tongue felt huge. I opened my mouth and showed Mom my bloody gums. Bishop O'Hara looked startled.

"Here," he said, drawing out his handkerchief and dangling it at me. "I've got some Kleenex in my office."

We followed him down a cold, dark corridor that ended in the most elegant office I've ever seen. On the ceiling a giant chandelier sparkled like a bushful of diamonds. The desk directly under it was so big that I could have tap-danced on it. A big gold box, a piece of marble with a pen sticking in it, and two typewriters sat on top of it. How can anybody use two typewriters? And pictures of people in halos, looking apologetic.

I lay down on a big leather sofa and pressed the bishop's handkerchief to my mouth.

"Cold water," he ordered Mom, and handed her Kleenex. "Go fetch cold water from the drinking fountain in the hall."

Mom ducked out, and he slippered over to me and folded his arms over his cassock.

"Now who really put that ball through the window?"

"My mom," I said.

He still didn't look convinced, so I explained that today was her final exam and Tristram was going to make us trash his marigolds if we lost. The bishop sighed deeply. I could see he was impressed.

"Is this her last lesson?"

I nodded.

"Good."

He didn't look so fierce to me now. Still, I was glad to see Mom bringing the cold water and the Kleenex. She handed him back his handkerchief and laid an icy-cold compress on my mouth. I didn't dare tell her it had stopped bleeding.

"I understand you've just finished your last baseball lesson, madam," said the bishop, addressing himself to a flower on the carpet.

"It better be," said Mom.

"Our Lord teaches us to forgive, not just seven times but seventy times seven."

Pause.

"Does that mean we don't have to pay a thousand dollars?" I asked.

"It means, don't ever play baseball around here again," said the bishop, and he wiped his handkerchief across his forehead. It left a thin streak of blood between his eyebrows. I sat up, completely cured.

"We won't, ever again," I promised.

Walking home, Mom and I didn't say much to

each other until we saw a little boy sitting behind a big box selling lemonade. The sign said:

FIVE CENTS FOR A DIRTY CUP
TEN CENTS FOR A CLEAN ONE

"I need a lemonade," said Mom. She laid down two dimes. "Two clean ones, please."

The boy rummaged around for a clean cup but found none.

"Make it four dirty ones," said Mom.

I drank one cup and Mom drank three, one right after the other.

"I'll take one more," said Mom.

The boy watched admiringly as she finished it off.

"You mighty thirsty," observed the boy. "You come from far away?"

"My mom and I been playing baseball," I said. "She's gonna be in the *Guinness Book of World Records.*"

"For drinking lemonade?" asked the boy. Mother was pouring herself a fifth.

"For hitting the highest ball," I answered.

Mom laid down another nickel, and he pocketed it.

"How high?" he asked, just as if Mom couldn't speak for herself. But I understood why she couldn't tell him. It's for us losers to praise the winners, not for the winners to praise themselves.

"She knocked off God's hat," I told him. "That's how high."

Five

WHEN BASEBALL SEASON ENDS
and school starts up again, I go back to my old job. I am
managing editor of *The Good Times,* which covers
mainly the neighborhood since I collect the news
myself, going from door to door. I keep it in the shoebox
under my bed where I keep my baseball cards. *The
Good Times* comes out whenever the box gets full.

If Mom's ditto machine is feeling up to it, Ellen
writes out the news on a master sheet while I page
through my *Believe It Or Not* for the fillers. As far as
I'm concerned, the fillers are the best part of the paper.
Not a day goes by you don't hear that Philip fell down
the cellar steps or Mrs. Bash's avocado plant has turned
over a new leaf. But a plant that catches a baseball, or a
man who wears the same clothes day and night for fifty
years, now that's worthy of notice.

What people don't know is that when I'm collect-
ing the news I'm also checking my traps. I have traps
hidden in almost all the neighbors' yards. I try to make
them look harmless, a box propped up by a stick with a
bit of carrot attached to it. You nibble the carrot and
down drops the box. There are a lot of rabbits in this
neighborhood, but I would settle for a raccoon. I know
I'll never get a pet of my own unless I catch it myself.
Whatever I catch I'll enter in the Rotary Club pet show
at the end of October. The judges give ribbons for the
smartest pet, the prettiest pet, the smallest pet, and the
biggest pet. If your pet wins two ribbons, you get a

watch, which I have wanted ever since Philip got one for his seventh birthday. Papa says he'll buy me one when I graduate from high school.

While my traps are out working for me, I keep a sharp eye on current events, in case I happen to see Dr. DeWigg's old shed burning down and I have to run in and save her two chickens. It's illegal to keep chickens in town, but she says they're a great comfort to her. She's ninety-nine, and Papa says she can get away with it.

Or maybe I'll spy the thief who broke into Jerry's shoe repair shop downtown and cleaned out his cashbox. And I won't ask Jerry for a reward, either, because he alone saves me the bottle caps from his Coke machine. All the other machines in town give cans.

I have about five traps set in the vacant lot next to Jerry's shop, right behind the old Dew Drop Inn. So when I saw somebody fixing up the inn, I was at once interested because nobody has gone near it since the New Players gave *The Devil and Daniel Webster.* Everybody who saw that play, including my mom, swore that when Daniel finished his big speech, he turned to the actor playing the Devil, and there right behind him stood the real Devil, glowing like a jack-o'-lantern. Nobody has set foot in the place since, and that happened two years ago.

Everybody wondered who was moving in, especially after two men came by and knocked a hole in the wall and put in a big window. Soon hair dryers appeared, and big chairs and a rubber plant.

"One more beauty shop," snorted Mrs. Bash. "This town has got five already."

Mrs. Bash runs the beauty shop on upper Main Street, and her married daughter runs the beauty shop on lower Main Street, and the ones in between, says Mrs. Bash, aren't worth bothering about. A girl in my class at school goes to Mrs. Bash's beauty shop every week and has her hair trimmed, washed, and baked. Not me. I never cut my hair, just pull it back in a rubber band and race out every morning, because I've got a lot to do, and like my piano teacher says, "Art is long but time is short."

One day a little sign appeared in the window of the new beauty shop.

SEBASTIAN'S MAGIC SHOP
go around the back.
Open   Sesame!

It was lettered in flames, all blowing to the left.

"Very sinister," Ellen said when she saw it. "I wouldn't go in that place for a hundred dollars."

The next afternoon I stopped by after school. A tall blonde woman with her hair piled up high was covering a lady's head with pincurls, and a girl about my size and wearing a Holy Cross jumper was sitting at a desk brushing pink polish on her nails. I let the door slam behind me, and she crossed her legs so that I would not fail to notice her white cowboy boots. She had long curly hair, redder than mine, which Mom calls red because brown sounds so mousy.

"Did you come for a perm?" she asked.

"I came to see the magic shop," I said.

"Well, you can't. Sebastian is fixing his stereo."

Seeing I was headed for the door, she added, "I've got my own horse. Also my own hair dryer. Also, I have seen the Liberty Bell."

"I've got a pet tree," I said. "A Norway maple."

She screwed the cap on the bottle of polish, and we told each other our names. Hers was Ursula Quinn.

"Come on," she said. She jumped up and pushed a path through a beaded curtain at the back of the shop. It rattled and clattered behind us. On the other side was a room full of furniture. Two TVs. Two washing machines, three sofas, a kitchen table, and a whole mob of chairs. A boy sprawled on the biggest sofa waved his sandwich at us. He looked a little like Philip, only scrawnier. He was watching the Monkees on both sets and chewing in time with the beat.

"Tony," said Ursula, "where's Sebastian? He's got a customer."

Tony slouched off the sofa, sidled toward a door at the back of the room, and disappeared.

"You sure got a lot of stuff," I said.

"Yeah. In Philadelphia our house was bigger. Do you want to see my room?"

It was small and cozy and done in wall-to-wall horses. There were horse heads on the bedspread and the curtains and horseshoes on the rug. Ursula hadn't made her bed, and that's how I found out about the racing horses on her sheets and her nightgown, which lay all mashed together in a pile on the floor. On a glass case stood about a hundred little china horses and a pile of movie magazines, the kind I am not allowed to read. Though I don't like horses that much, I liked the room.

"Look," said Ursula and she pulled up her skirt to show me the horses printed on her underpants. "My mom got me these last week for my birthday. And my dad sent me this box of soap."

The box was painted like a stable. Across the roof it said that the five white horses inside were guaranteed nontoxic to the most sensitive skin.

Ursula opened a door that looked like a closet. "The bathroom," she announced. "Ta-ta!"

The toilet seat had a horse on it, all saddled.

"My dad sent this for my brother Thomas. He does poo in his diapers if he can't sit on the horse."

"How many brothers do you have?" I asked.

"Five," said Ursula. And she counted them on her fingers. "Sebastian, Anthony, Thomas, Stephen, and Joseph."

The way she rattled off those names made them sound like a magic spell. I didn't believe she had that many.

"Where are they?" I asked.

"Stephen and Joseph are in the army. Thomas is at the sitter's."

Suddenly voices rose and fell from the other side of the wall I was leaning on.

"Come on," said Ursula. "The magic shop is open."

She pushed me back into the living room and through a door just behind the TVs. The magic shop looked as bare as a church basement. There was nothing to browse over but a pamphlet rack. It showed mostly titles like *So You Want to Be a Magician* and *Best Card Tricks Ever* and *Eating Fire for Fun and Profit*.

You could see right away that Sebastian was keeping all the good stuff in his glass showcase, under lock and key. Tony was lounging against the glass, feeding his sandwich crusts to a lovely blue parakeet in a bamboo cage that swung from a hook on the ceiling.

"Show her some tricks, Sebastian," said Tony to the tall sly-faced boy behind the counter.

Sebastian never cracked a smile, no doubt for fear of leaking one of his thousands of secrets.

"You a beginner?" he asked.

"Yeah," I admitted. Behind the glass, wands and rings and paper flowers were laid out as neatly as a surgeon's instruments.

"What's your name?"

"Kate."

"I got a good trick here for beginners, Kate. It's a cup of coffee that shakes by itself."

He reached into the case, pulled out a very homely cup and saucer, and smirked.

"Now when somebody pours in the coffee, watch."

Tony poured in the last of his milk. Suddenly the cup began to quake till it nearly leaped out of Sebastian's hand. I knew it would scare Mom out of her wits because she's always saying she drinks too much coffee, but I am kindhearted. Besides, it cost two dollars and twenty-five cents.

"How does it work?" I asked.

Sebastian shook his head. "Buy the trick, and I'll show you the secret."

I never learned the secret because I bought a book

on fire-eating instead. It was two dollars cheaper, and after I read it I plan on giving it to Trudy, who is always sneaking smokes around the old lady she sometimes works for when she's not keeping an eye on me. I laid my quarter on the counter, and Sebastian slapped it down like it was a flea.

"Always wish on the first money of the day," he grinned. "For ten cents more, you can buy a ticket to see the Great Escapo. One of the greatest magicians of all time. One o'clock next Saturday at the public library."

He waited for me to fall on my knees.

"That show is free," said Ursula. "You got your nerve, Sebastian."

Far off I heard the five o'clock whistle from the cough-drop factory across town. Papa sets his watch by that whistle.

"I got to go home," I said.

"Oh, not yet," said Ursula. "We've just met. Can't you stay for supper?"

"What's for supper?" asked Tony.

"Corn flakes," announced Ursula. "Mom's keeping the beauty shop open till seven tonight. You can help me set the table, Kate."

And she bustled out of the magic shop, turned off the TV, and started setting up TV tables in front of all the overstuffed chairs. Then she fetched the milk and the bowls and spoons.

"Let's you and Tony and me eat. We don't have to wait for the others," she said.

I knew I should have gone home, but it didn't seem polite to leave.

"Pretty nice," I said. "Everybody has a private table."

Ursula counted them once more. "Yeah, it's nice. Only sometimes I wish we could sit down all together and say grace."

Tony put the bird cage carefully on the TV, right by his table. "This bird is very smart," he informed me. "She does the rhumba. Watch."

He poked his spoon through the bars of the cage, and the parakeet darted to and fro on her perch in a panic. Anybody would.

"Are you going to enter her in the Rotary Club pet show?" I asked.

"Gonna enter her as the smartest pet. Gonna win, too," said Tony. Every word he spoke sounded as if it had dust on it. "First prize is a watch," he added.

"You have three watches already," said Ursula. "What do you want with another one?"

"Gonna sell it," said Tony. "Gonna save all my money till I get a thousand-dollar bill. The government makes 'em, you know."

For a few minutes we ate our corn flakes in silence. I had seconds and poured on so much milk they crackled at me, and then Ursula poured me more corn flakes to take up the milk. I've seen my dad finish a whole box of cereal that way, from flakes to milk, from milk to flakes, on and on, to the bottom of the box.

"I should be getting home," I said, and I tried to

stand up, but Tony pushed me down.

"I'm so good in gym that the school has put me in a special class," he said. "You want to see my thumb muscles?"

"No," said Ursula.

"You want to hear my CB radio? I get Mars on it sometimes."

If the Rotary Club ever gives watches to the kid who can tell the biggest lie, I will write Tony up in my paper. But until that day comes, I don't go in for lies, because _The Good Times_ only prints the truth.

I turned my attention to Ursula, who I figured was my real competition for a watch. "Where's your horse?" I asked her.

"My horse is back home in Philly," said Ursula. "A man boards her for me. When we lived close to the stables, I used to get up every morning and groom her myself. At night in summer I'd sleep in her stall. Now I only get to ride her when I visit my dad."

"Why do you have to visit him?" I asked.

"Divorce," she said. "My folks are divorced."

"How terrible—" I blurted out. "I mean," I added hastily, "for some people it's terrible."

Actually I was thinking of my cousin, who is just my age. When his mom got a divorce, he got attacks of asthma and hives.

Ursula wasn't listening. "Do you have a horse?" she asked.

"No. And I don't have a bird, either. My parents won't buy me a pet because Mom says she doesn't want to end up taking care of it."

"I bet you wish you had a horse," said Ursula. "Tell you what. Maybe my dad can win you one, too."

A wave of happiness washed over me. "How did he win her?" I asked.

"Oh, he didn't win *her*. He won the money to buy her at the races. When we lived in Philly, he used to take me to the track every Saturday after my catechism class. Tony, get your ear out of Kate's corn flakes."

"I'm listening to your corn flakes, Kate," said Tony. "I can understand every word corn flakes say."

"What do my corn flakes say?" I asked him, very curious.

He lifted his head. "Do you speak Spanish?" he inquired.

I told him I didn't.

"Sorry," said Tony, "but your corn flakes only speak Spanish."

Down the street, the bell at Holy Cross rang for Vespers, slowly and sadly.

"I'm leaving," I said and stood up fast.

"I'll walk you to the end of the block," said Ursula.

In the beauty shop, half a dozen women dozed under the dryers. Next door, Jerry was working late, too; we could hear the rumble of the big machine that he uses to stitch body and sole together, he says. He waved at us, and the black cat painted on his window waved, too, in honor of Cat's Paw heels, which Jerry highly recommends.

We passed Holy Cross school and the church beside it. I could see the shadow of the big bell moving in the high tower, though it had stopped ringing.

"My brothers go to Holy Cross," observed Ursula.

"So do you," I said.

"Only to the school. On Sundays Mom takes me to Saint Andrew's Episcopal."

"We're Quakers," I said.

"Are you the people that roll on the floor?" inquired Ursula.

"I don't think so," I answered. "I've never seen anyone roll on the floor during Meeting."

A dreamy look crossed Ursula's face. I could tell she wasn't listening.

"Have you ever worn a bra?" she asked suddenly.

That surprised me. "Flat as an ironing board," Ellen calls me.

"No," I said, "have you?"

"Meet me tomorrow after school at Kresge's for the chance of a lifetime."

Six

KRESGE'S WAS JAMMED. ON A
cold day a lot of people go in there just to warm up.
Paper Santa Clauses fluttered from the ceiling, and we
hadn't even got to Halloween yet.

"Ursula," I said, "I'm not going to try on anything
in front of a hundred people."

"You don't have to," said Ursula. "Any place that
sells underwear has a fitting room." She motioned me to
follow her. "Counter five. Come on."

The bras and underpants lay on the counter in
shriveled heaps. Ursula looked around to make sure
nobody she knew was watching. Then her hand darted
forth and fished something out of the pile. It was large,
black lace, ribbed, and it glittered like a padded bird
cage. The saleslady's face rose like a moon over the top
of the counter. Wire-rimmed glasses, short blond hair.
She stood at attention by the cash register.

"Is this a bra or a corset?" asked Ursula.

"That," said the clerk, "is a Merry Widow."

I was struck dumb with admiration. Even with
nobody inside, it still stuck out in all the right places.

"It looks uncomfortable," said Ursula.

"Mmmm," said the clerk. "But it really lifts you—
here." She pushed up a huge wad of air with her hands.

"Is there a place we can try it on?" asked Ursula.

"The fitting booth is right over there, next to the
pet department."

"I'll go first," whispered Ursula. "You act as decoy.

If you see anybody we know, lure them away."

The fitting room was a couple of shower curtains hung from a big ring on the back wall, pulled around a little pinch of floor between the aquariums and the parakeet cages. Ursula disappeared behind the curtains, and I stationed myself in front of the biggest cage and exchanged hellos with a bright green parrot.

"Hey, Kate!"

Ursula stuck her head out and grinned. "You won't believe what this does for you. It'll take me a few minutes to unhook, though."

Suddenly she turned pale.

"It's him!" she shrieked and ducked behind the curtain.

"Who? Who?" I cried.

"Father Beasley," said Ursula's voice. It sounded all trembly. "What's he doing in the dime store?"

"Who's Father Beasley?" I asked.

"He's the rector at Saint Andrew's. He's lots nicer than Father Flannagan at Holy Cross. He's young."

Two counters away I saw a small man with a pointed beard and red hair that sprang out from either side of his head in two bunches.

"If he's so young, why is he wearing a wig?"

"That's not a wig. His hair grows in tufts," said Ursula. "What's more, he suffered a great tragedy when he was eighteen. My mom told me." There was silence in the booth. Then Ursula whispered. "It was unrequited love. Listen, Kate. Go and see what he's buying."

"Go and see for yourself," I told her.

"I can't. He knows me. Oh, Kate, I'll let you wear

my Saint Anthony medal for your next math test. My dad gave it to me, and it's twenty-four-karat gold. It was blessed by the Pope."

I knew she would have promised me anything at that moment, but I couldn't think of a single thing to ask for. And then I thought, maybe someday it'll be me begging for some great favor. Like Philip's mom says, you never know on which side of the fence you'll find yourself.

"Hurry," said Ursula. "He might leave."

I walked over and stood next to Father Beasley. He was buying pajamas. He split open a package, pulled out one sleeve, and twitched it between his fingers. He had taken off one glove. His hand was a peculiar white like piano keys, and his neck was very red above his collar, as if his mother had just scrubbed it. The elderly saleslady on the other side of the counter watched him as patiently as I did.

I sidled closer. Half a book peeped out from his overcoat pocket—*Is Hell Real?* I made a point of remembering the title for Ursula.

The saleslady looked from Father Beasley to the pajamas. "And they're flame retardant, Father," she said at last.

Something small and white fluttered from the glove he was holding. A piece of paper. I picked it up and popped it into my pocket. A little treasure for Ursula.

The saleslady turned to me. "Can I help you?"

I thought fast. "Socks," I said. "My dad wears socks."

"What size?"

I didn't know what size, as I always buy him handkerchiefs. So I said the first number that came into my head. "Twenty," I said. "He wears size twenty."

Father Beasley looked up in surprise, then he looked down in alarm. Then he began shuffling through all the pajamas. "It's gone," he told the clerk.

"What's gone?" she asked.

"My lottery ticket. I had it in my glove."

The saleslady's face remained as set as cement. "Are you sure about the size?" she asked me severely.

"I don't know," I said. "Let me walk around the block and think about it."

I hurried back to Ursula in the fitting booth.

"What's he buying?" she asked, from behind drawn curtains.

"Pajamas," I said.

"What color?"

"Blue striped."

"Oh, Kate," said Ursula, "did you notice the size?"

"Now, would I notice the size?"

"Go back and look. Oh, please, Kate, I'll give you my Galway ring."

I've always wanted a gold ring. This one had two hands clasping a heart where other rings have stones.

"You'll really give me your ring?"

"Yes, if you promise to give it back."

I didn't mind helping her. But when I went back to the pajama counter, Father Beasley was gone.

When Ursula heard this, she came out.

"Father Beasley lost his lottery ticket," I said, "but I saved it. For you." And I uncrumpled it in her hand.

She gazed at it tenderly for several minutes.

"I'll return it," she said, and I could tell that she had almost decided not to. "I'll put it in the envelope with his gum."

"His gum?"

"I always buy gum with my allowance, and I leave it in his mailbox. Of course I never leave my name," she added. She handed me the Merry Widow. "Your turn."

I hesitated.

"Oh, Kate, it's the chance of a lifetime."

I pulled the curtain around me. From inside the fitting booth I could hear the parakeets jumping from perch to perch. Through a crack in the curtains I could see their cages swing back and forth on tall stands. The water in the fish tanks gurgled noisily. I pulled off my mittens, plopped my coat on the floor, stepped out of my skirt, and pulled off my blue sweater. I hung my sweater over the top of the curtain so it wouldn't fall into the fish water or over a cage. Then I took a deep breath and wrapped the Merry Widow around myself and started hooking it down the back. The big stay at the center cut into my chest, but this was the chance of a lifetime, and I stuck with it. At my left ear, the parakeets whistled, and two women I couldn't see argued about underwear.

"Fifteen pairs!" said one. "You think you're going on your honeymoon?"

"Listen, honey, the elastic is shot on everything I own, and I'm all chafed," said the other woman. "For ninety-nine cents, why should I suffer?"

"That blue sweater would fit Sandy," said the first

woman, "but there's no price on it. Isn't it awful how people just leave merchandise lying around on the floor?"

I pulled one hook too far, and the whole garment snapped at me. Took my breath clean away. The center stay split my little gold locket into neat halves, like a lima bean. I took off the Merry Widow before worse happened, and I put on my skirt. Then I reached up for my blue sweater.

Gone.

Crouching down, I peered under the curtain to see if it had dropped to the floor. Nothing. I figured it must have got stuck on the way down. I reached my hand through the curtain and pawed the air till it bumped against something.

"Mind your purse!" shrieked a voice. "Thief!"

Somebody started frisking the fitting booth. I grabbed my coat and crawled under the curtain. As I pushed my way clear, I heard a tremendous crash.

When I came up for air, two salesladies were waving fishnets and chasing birds. The parakeet cages lay prostrate across the aisle. Nobody noticed me except Ursula, who was standing in the middle of the aisle with her mouth hanging open.

"Let's go," I said, buttoning my coat to the chin.

"Where?"

"Home. Somebody stole my sweater. My mom will have a fit."

When we got outside, Ursula laid a soothing hand on my arm. "I'll give you one of my sweaters. Your mom will think we've traded. Let me treat you to some gum at Woolworth's."

The gum machine at Woolworth's is a crystal globe, and it never runs dry. You put in your penny and you hold your hand under the spout. You always get gum. If you're lucky, you also get a charm. Last Monday I counted twenty plastic four-leaf clovers, eight thimbles, five skulls that glow in the dark, and a diamond ring that was pressing its face to the glass and sparkling its heart out.

"If I get the diamond ring," said Ursula, "you can borrow it."

I figured it was a show of generosity in case God was listening. Clunk! went the coin. We watched a hundred gumballs shift their weight, like people letting someone off the bus at rush hour.

"What'd you get?" I asked carelessly.

"Gum," said Ursula. "Your turn." She shook the gum into her glove.

I got a handful of gum and a four-leaf clover with one leaf bitten off. I wrapped the gum in the Kleenex Mom hides in all my pockets, and I threw the clover in the trash can. Then we went to Ursula's house and headed straight for her horsey bedroom, where she gave me her navy sweater with a moth hole in the elbow. It fit me all right. And I could mend the hole.

"Let's go see the Frankenstein movie at the public library tomorrow after school," I said. "We can meet on the playground and take the bus downtown."

"Mmm," said Ursula. "I've got a lot of homework. But I'll call you tonight and let you know if I'm going." I could tell she wasn't listening to me but to the bells in the clock tower at Holy Cross. "It's four o'clock. That's when he goes to Thompson's luncheonette for a cup of coffee."

"Who?" I said.

"Father Beasley."

"Him again! How do you know where he goes?" I asked.

"I know everything he does," said Ursula. "I mean, everything he does regularly. I've got his whole life inside my head like a movie. In the morning, when I'm chewing my Cheerios, I can see him chewing his Cheerios."

A chill passed over me at so much secrecy and intrigue. "How do you know he eats Cheerios?" I asked.

"Sebastian delivers his groceries. Every week he delivers twenty-five lemon yogurts. How can one man eat twenty-five yogurts in a week?"

"He must be on a diet," I said.

"And I always thought he liked strawberry best," said Ursula. "Save me all your lemon gumballs, okay? Sebastian gave me a very good account of the kitchen." She frowned. "I wish I knew what the rest of his house looks like. I suppose it's all brown, like the Sunday school parlor. Big old chairs. Huge tables."

I eased my way over to the door.

"I've got to go home. Don't forget to call me about *Frankenstein*."

"I've heard," said Ursula mysteriously, "of a great

way to get a fabulous bust."

My hand slipped off the doorknob, and I came back. "What is it?" I asked.

"The main piece of equipment is a vacuum cleaner."

She jumped up and ran into the next room, where I heard her crashing around in her mother's closet. Soon she returned dragging a vacuum cleaner by its neck like a dead goose. Over her arm she carried one of her mother's bras. Black.

Ursula plugged in the vacuum cleaner and snapped it on and darted the nozzle across the rug. A paper clip crackled out of sight. A postage stamp gave up the ghost. She turned it off.

"How does it give you a fabulous bust?" I asked.

"You put the nozzle on your chest and turn it on," said Ursula.

I thought about the paper clip and the postage stamp. "I don't think I want to try it first," I said.

Ursula didn't either. She put on the bra over her middy shirt and appraised herself in the mirror.

"You could stuff them with socks," I suggested. "That way, if you wanted more, you could add more socks. If you wanted less—"

Then Tony hurled himself into the room, and we hid everything.

Seven

WHEN I GOT HOME, ELLEN WAS
sitting in the dining room doing her homework, and
Trudy was sitting in the living room watching TV and
waiting for her taxi.

"Ursula phoned," said Trudy. "She says she does
want to go with you to see *Frankenstein*. She'll meet
you at Holy Cross."

"Remember to get back in time to help Mom clean
the house for Dr. DeWigg's party tomorrow," called
Ellen. "She's going to be a hundred years old. You
ought to make her a card."

I took out my gumballs, and the Kleenex split.

"Have some gum," I shouted over the rolling and
the clattering.

"Fetch a broom," Trudy shouted back. "Stepping
on a gumball is worse'n stepping on a marble."

I swept my gumballs into a big pile on the rug and
then picked out all the yellow ones.

"What you got against yellow?" asked Trudy.

"Ursula saves all the yellow gumballs for Father
Beasley. Lemon's his favorite flavor. What's yours?"

"Cherry," said Trudy, and she lifted her upper lip
and licked the tip of her nose. She says she is the only
woman in America who can do this, and she has to keep
practicing so as not to lose the touch. I was on the point
of offering her my cherry gumballs, but what I saw
stopped me.

"Where are your teeth?" I asked.

"In my purse. I'm resting 'em. Father Beasley—I think I seen him at Thompson's. My cousin works at Thompson's. Does he have horns?"

"Those are not horns," I said. "Those are tufts. His hair grows in two tufts."

She didn't say anything right away. I could tell she was thinking about tufts. "You ever seen anyone else with tufts?" she asked.

"Dagwood," called Ellen from the dining room.

"I don't say he's got horns," added Trudy. "I just say that *if* you had horns, tufts would be a very convenient place to hide 'em."

"Don't forget tomorrow's also paper day," came Ellen's voice again from the next room. "Did you collect the news yet?"

I grabbed my notebook and ran over to Philip's house. His mom has more news than all the rest of us put together. The front door wasn't locked, so I walked right in. Philip lay stretched out on the living room floor. He was watching TV with his Dracula mask on. I could hear his mom shouting to Mrs. Bull in the kitchen, so I headed for the kitchen.

"Shake it!" Mrs. Bull was yelling.

When they saw me they quieted down. They were holding a huge turkey and peering up into its empty stomach. Suddenly a bar of soap dropped out.

"You're the only person I know that soaps her turkey," observed Mrs. Bull.

"Parrot fever," said Philip's mom. "Remember that hotel in Philadelphia where so many people died of a mysterious disease? My brother says it was parrot fever.

Not just parrots carry it, either. Anyone can carry it."

She plopped the turkey into the sink, rinsed out its stomach, and ran a wad of butter up and down its skin, like a chill. I got goose bumps just watching her.

"Mrs. Fitzpatrick, do you have any news?" I asked.

"Lesseee. What did I do today, Janet?"

"You took Philip to the doctor's," said Mrs. Bull.

"I took Philip to the doctor's. His cast comes off next week."

"My cast comes off next week," sang Philip, who would waken from a dead sleep if you stood on the far side of Mars and murmured his name.

Three weeks ago Tristram pushed him out of a tree. Now Philip stood in the doorway and held up his broken arm in its cast like a water pipe. It was papered with all the Chiquita banana seals he'd been saving for the last three years.

"Take off that mask," said his mother. "We have company." He pulled it off, but slowly, and a red spot the size of a fifty-cent piece glowed on his left cheek. Both mothers leaned forward.

"It looks like ringworm," said Mrs. Fitzpatrick.

"I got it from Walter on the bus," said Philip.

"Walter has ringworm?" cried Mrs. Bull.

"Walter bit me," said Philip. "But he won't do it again, because there's an invisible jail on the bus. The driver says so."

"I'm going gray, simply gray," moaned Mrs. Fitzpatrick. "Last week he fell off the cannon in front of the public library and cracked his head open."

"I had to have stitches," said Philip.

"How many?" I asked. So far I have had eight, which is the record for our neighborhood, and I've saved them all, plus the five my dad got when he split his finger playing basketball.

"Two," said Philip. "Here."

He turned around and lifted the hair at the back of his neck, revealing a little shaved square, trussed in cross-stitch, like a football.

"And the week before he fell out of bed and cut his neck on the radiator valve."

Philip lifted his chin and pointed to a small scar, but it had nearly healed out of sight.

"Inches away from the jugular," observed Mrs. Bull.

"And the week before, he wore his Frankenstein fangs to Communion. Lord, what I have to suffer."

I figured I had enough right there for the whole front page.

"Got to be running along," I said. "See you tomorrow, Philip."

Nobody said good-bye. On the way home I stopped to check the trap in their back yard. The box was still balanced on its stick, and nobody had so much as nibbled the carrot I'd laid underneath.

As I was crossing our back yard, I could see Mom through the screen door, standing in front of the open refrigerator and gazing hopefully into it as if she'd just been told five minutes before that she had to prepare dinner for four. Every evening she makes this amazing discovery. She caught sight of me.

"If you're going to Dr. DeWigg's," she shouted, "ask her for a cutting from her prayer plant. Mine died."

There was nothing in the trap I'd set in Dr. DeWigg's asparagus patch, so I went up to the front porch and rang the bell. Betty Rout, the girl who helps take care of the house, opened the door.

"Oh, it's you," she said, obviously disappointed.

I didn't mind. I have heard that her boy friend always arrives without notice.

"Do you have any news?" I asked.

She thought for a moment and said, "The doctor took her constitutional at ten o'clock this morning. She walked to the end of the veranda and back."

I wrote it down. I write it down every week the same.

"And the doctor's cat took *her* constitutional at eleven o'clock. From here to the apple tree," said Betty.

"And back," I added.

"No," said Betty. "I have to carry her back. She's nineteen years old. In cat years that makes her over a hundred."

"Can I have a sprig of the doctor's prayer plant?"

"Another one?"

I tiptoed after her into the living room. The house is so still you can hear the cat's toenails scraping on the wooden floor above the bubbling of the aquarium. The window sills are full of sea shells and salt shakers and geraniums, and the room is always cool, even in the middle of July. Dr. DeWigg was lying on her chaise listening to the radio.

"Who is it?" she asked.

"It's me," I answered, and I hurried over to where she could see me.

She put on her glasses to be sure. Then she said in her tiny crisp voice, "Kate, be sure to bring your mother a sprig of my prayer plant."

Next to Dr. DeWigg's is Hildegarde Bash's house. It's also her husband's, but she does all the work on it. I can't keep a trap in her yard because she has rid herself of grass forever and put in white stones, which she hoses down every afternoon, except in winter. Every time I stop by, she tells me she is trying to convert Mr. Bash to a life of hard work and ambition. He doesn't work regularly, but he's a very good tap dancer, and he can sing Al Jolson's greatest hits in a way that melts your heart. Once when Mrs. Bash let me use the bathroom, I discovered a marvelous bar of soap, shaped like a microphone and painted gray, with a cord on it, for singing in the shower. Mr. Bash has plans for extensive traveling, he tells me, when he's worked up a couple of good routines.

Mrs. Bash's head appeared over the top of the roof. She was waving a hammer, and her mouth was full of nails.

"Have you got any news?" I hollered up at her.

She spit out the nails like cherry pits. "Nope," she hollered back.

"Any want ads?"

She thought for a moment. "Justin needs an alarm clock. He's been complaining all week that nobody ever says good morning to him. I tell him, how can anyone say good morning to a man who don't rise before noon?"

I saved Mr. Goldberg for last, the way I like to save the frosting on a piece of cake for the last bite. He's seventy-five, and he always invites me in for a chat and treats me like a grown-up. I fetch him a can of beer from the refrigerator—"Pour it in that thin-lipped glass, Kate, so it tastes good"—and a bottle of grape soda for me, which I drink from a big mug, with lots of ice. He saves me his Yiddish newspapers and the labels from his matzoh boxes, because he knows I like to copy the Hebrew letters. They are so beautiful it gives my hand pleasure just to write them.

In exchange for these services, I return his library books for him so he can make his morning expedition to the library "with a light heart and empty hands," and he only has to carry the new books home. What a grand sight he makes, tossing his cane in the air like a baton. I love that cane. It has a dog's head carved on the handle, set with real glass eyes. Sitting across from him, I wondered why he kept it leaning against his chair, just as if he couldn't walk without it.

"Where did you get your cane?" I asked.

"That cane," said Mr. Goldberg, "is of unknown origin. Like me. Most remarkable things are, you know."

"Is that what 'of unknown origin' means? Something remarkable?"

He nodded and grinned.

"You walk okay without a cane," I went on, "so why do you carry it?"

"For dancing," said Mr. Goldberg.

"You ought to loan it to Mr. Bash. He's a good tap dancer. You should see him dance 'The Taxicab.' "

Mr. Goldberg snorted. "He learned how to tap-dance from me. I used to dance 'The Huckle Buck' in a straw hat with Maurice Chevalier." His lips twitched into a smile. "Do you believe me?"

"Sort of," I said. I never know whether to believe him or not, especially when he tells me stories of his exciting youth.

"Did I ever tell you how I wrestled alligators for Ringling Brothers?"

"No."

"You got to grab their jaws. Once an alligator snapped off my watch and ate it. A waterproof, shockproof Timex."

The loss of a watch seemed too terrible even to speak of.

"You never got it back?"

"I got this new one." He held out his wrist. His watch ticked up at me, cunning, obedient, and shiny. All my old longings flooded over me. He turned its face over.

"I want a watch more than anything," I confessed. "Why do you wear yours with the face turned down?"

"So I don't have to see what time it is." He sipped his beer for several minutes, then set down his glass. "You don't need a watch."

"Yes, I do."

I told him my plans for entering the pet show, if I could just catch myself a pet. He sat very still, listening. For a few minutes, neither of us spoke.

At last Mr. Goldberg broke the silence. "I used to keep an alligator in my bathtub. Now, do you believe that?"

"Yes," I said.

"Why?"

"Because you said it."

Mr. Goldberg gave a great hoot. "That's what I love about you kids," he exclaimed. "You believe anything. Now grownups, they'll say, 'Was it a real alligator?' 'Did you really keep it in a bathtub? It could have been a fake.' The minute you catch yourself saying, 'It could have been a fake,' you'll know you're growing up."

Suddenly his mouth looked sad.

"I'll always believe everything," I promised him.

He sipped his beer and I sipped my grape soda and just felt happy. Someday I'd like to explore his house and see if the other rooms are as mysterious as his living room. Old minnow nets and bait cans in the corners, old newspapers stacked to the ceiling. I figured it was nearly time to talk about his wife, which is what we do when we finish our drinks. She died ten years ago, but he talks about her as if she'd just stepped out to the store.

"I saw Rachel last night," said Mr. Goldberg. "Wonderful, wonderful. We lose sight of each other, but we find each other again."

That startled me, I can tell you. "Where'd you see her?" I asked.

"In a dream. How lucky I am to have dreams! After she died I thought I'd never see her again. Last night we were walking on the road to our village in Poland, the way it used to be. The fields, all wheat and poppies. No cars. It was summer. But I was freezing to death. 'Sure is hot,' said Rachel, and she gave me her coat. So I put on her coat. 'Look at the flowers,' she said. 'Just like Florida.' "

"Is Florida where you wrestled the alligators?" I asked. I like to keep my facts straight.

"That's the place," said Mr. Goldberg. "And then Rachel and I had an argument. You know, she was always a heavy woman. She died of a heart attack, talking on the telephone. Just dropped right over. Two hours before she died, she wanted a chocolate pudding for lunch. I told her, 'You can't have that pudding. You got to watch your weight.' Now every time I see her, she yells at me, 'Why didn't you let me eat that pudding, seeing as I only had two hours left to go?' We always argued a lot," he said, and his mouth looked sad again.

"So do the Bashes," I said.

"Guess everybody does," said Mr. Goldberg. "Did you catch anything in your traps yet?"

I laughed. Because when I'm talking with him, I forget about the traps, the news, everything.

"If I ever go back to Florida, I'll send you an indigo snake," he said, as I got up to go. "They're gorgeous. You'd win first prize in any pet show with one of them."

Through the open window came the *ooom pah pah* of Ellen practicing the bottom half of our duet. Mom was out in the front yard raking the grass to pieces, the way she does when she's worried about me.

"Where were you?"

"Getting the news."

"Have you done your homework? And what about your practicing? The recital is only one week off."

"Is Papa home yet? I'm starved."

I walked slowly when I got inside. I have nothing against practicing, but the piano is across the room, and it takes me a long time to get there. I can touch anything but the rug. If I touch the rug, I'm a nerd.

Ellen had left the living room, so I sat down at the piano and fished a card out of the bowl where Mom keeps the practicing rewards. Walt Frazier! The first basketball card of the season. I opened my music book with a glad heart.

Eight

WHEN I WOKE UP, I KNEW I WAS looking at the perfect day for *Frankenstein*. Mom was moaning like a vampire in the kitchen, trying to phone the dentist. Outside my window: gray sky, bare trees. And the sky stayed gray all day.

After school I ran straight up the hill to Holy Cross. Ursula was standing by the empty field, holding herself aloof from the swarms of kids that wrestled and yelled as they waited for their rides.

"Let's take the bus downtown to the library," I suggested.

"No," said Ursula, who loves to ride the bus. "Let's walk."

That saddened me. I love to ride the bus, too. Sometimes I just ride it for fun, from my part of town to everybody else's and back again.

"After the movie, let's go to Woolworth's and get our pictures taken," I said.

"Only if we can get back before dark," said Ursula. "I can't stay downtown after dark."

It gets dark early since we set our clocks back for daylight saving time. Mom says she wishes whoever is saving it would give her some. Ursula trudged along beside me in silence while I cheered her with the stories from *Believe It Or Not* that I'm saving for the next issue of *The Good Times*. I told her in great detail about the man in Scotland who towed a dead whale with one hand for ten miles. Then I told her about the man who could quote the entire Bible from memory, starting at any chapter or verse, but could never remember his children's names.

Suddenly Ursula jerked to a stop and clutched her neck. "Agggh!" she cried.

"What's wrong with you?" I exclaimed, drawing back.

"My neck," squeaked Ursula. "It's stiffened up. See, I can only turn it so far."

She turned it so far.

"You mean your neck is stuck?" I asked. I had never heard of such a thing, but I didn't want to alarm her.

"It's stuck," she groaned. "I'll have to go and get it healed right away."

She didn't look as scared as I thought she should.

"Where do you go to get it healed?" I inquired, hoping the place wasn't too far off.

A dreamy expression dropped like a veil over Ursula's face. "Father Beasley has a special service to heal the sick on Wednesdays at three o'clock. What time is it?"

By a remarkable coincidence, we had arrived at Saint Andrew's, which is Father Beasley's church. The clock in the steeple said three o'clock.

"Now isn't that the most convenient thing you ever heard of," said Ursula.

"Does that mean we can't see *Frankenstein?*" I asked.

"How can I sit through *Frankenstein* with my neck stuck?" she whined.

She hadn't slowed her pace during this awful discovery, and we now found ourselves at the church door.

"Come in with me," she pleaded. "I'm scared to go alone."

I had a feeling things were not as they appeared to be, but there wasn't time to sort it all out now. So I followed her into the vestibule, past the pamphlet rack, and through the heavy doors into the sanctuary. It was dark and filled with mutterings. A perfect place to see *Frankenstein.* About half a dozen old women huddled together in a pew near the front.

"Hardly anybody's here," I whispered.

"Sshhhh," hissed Ursula. "We'll sit near the middle."

Suddenly Father Beasley flitted in and lit the candles, circling the altar like a moth. I thought of him in the dime store, studying the blue striped pajamas, and he didn't look so spooky.

The prayers unrolled like the longest ribbon in the world. There were some nice parts about lions and plagues, but pretty soon I wished I had something to color or read. And just as I'd made up my mind to walk out and leave Ursula to unkink her own neck, Father Beasley turned to us and intoned:

"The Almighty Lord, Who is a most strong tower to all who trust in Him, be now and evermore your defense and make you know the only Name given for health and salvation is the Name of our Lord Jesus Christ. Let those who wish to be healed come forward."

Ursula sat up very straight. Her face was as pale as

paper. The little knot of women in the pew ahead of us rose and surged forward like a delegation.

"What's happening?" I whispered.

"I'm scared," gasped Ursula. "I'm scared to go up. Come with me."

"Me! I have nothing wrong with me."

"Nobody's perfect," she snapped. "You must have something wrong with you. Think."

I thought. I thought of *Frankenstein*. Maybe with so few of us here, Father Beasley would let us out in time for the second reel.

"Your wart," exclaimed Ursula, jerking my pony tail to one side and studying my neck. "Didn't you tell me you had a wart on your neck?"

I pulled away from her. "My mom says nobody should touch anybody else's warts. They're catching."

"Don't you have any others?" asked Ursula.

"Just one," I said, "on my big toe." I wondered if a blessing could cut through all the dirt and calluses on the soles of my feet. Trudy says I should send a letter about my feet to *Believe It Or Not* and tell them I am growing my own shoes.

The women knelt by the altar railing, and Father Beasley hurried down the whole row, laying his hands on their heads and murmuring. Then he glanced out at us.

Ursula nudged me and stood up, and we inched forward, solemn as crows. Father Beasley's hand on my hair felt as warm and heavy as a sleeping cat.

"I lay my hand upon you in the name of the Father, and of the Son, and of the Holy Spirit:

beseeching the mercy of our Lord Jesus Christ, that, putting to flight all sickness of body and spirit, He may give you the victory of life and peace which will help you to serve Him both now and evermore. Amen."

Next he laid his hand on Ursula's bangs. She was leaning against the rail as though she were going to faint away.

When the service ended, she didn't look much better for it. She went in clutching her neck, and she went out clutching her head.

"He touched me!" she shouted. "Right here! I'm never going to wash the spot as long as I live! Let me treat you to a Coke at Jerry's."

I don't like drinking Cokes at Jerry's. Who wants to make merry with hundreds of old shoes sticking out their tongues at you? Through the window of the shoe shop, Jerry's bald head bobbed over the top of his electric polisher. He was putting up a sign. He has papered his shop with signs designed to answer any question you might want to ask, since the polisher and the stitching machine make such a clatter you can't hear the sound of your own voice.

"DO YOU THINK FATHER BEASLEY NO-TICED MY HAIR?" she shouted as she handed me a Coke. "MOM SET IT LAST NIGHT."

I nodded and sipped.

"I WISH I COULD MAKE HIM SOMETHING TO WEAR. YOU ALWAYS MAKE SUCH NICE PRESENTS FOR PEOPLE."

I nodded again. This did not seem the time to

explain that my mom requires me to knit three inches every day on the stockings I am making for Ellen's birthday or go without dessert.

Jerry stood back and admired his sign. Among the shoes, boots, magazines, and framed photographs of his mother, it was hardly noticeable. But you could see it pleased him.

> *If you come for good work, you have come to the right place. But! If you came to argue or harass, you have come to the wrong place. There is too much fighting in the world. Let us all do our part to make it peaceful.*

"I WISH I'D GET IN AN ACCIDENT AND FATHER BEASLEY WOULD HAVE TO SAVE ME," roared Ursula over the din. "I MEAN, MAYBE I COULD GET HIT BY A CAR, BUT NOT SO BAD THAT I'D NEED STITCHES. JUST A LITTLE BLOOD. A COUPLE OF SCRAPED KNEES."

Jerry slipped around the edge of the counter and waved a shoebox of bottlecaps at me.

"Just for you," he mouthed.

"Thanks," I mouthed back.

We finished our Cokes and headed outside for the bus stop. On the way we passed Father Beasley's big old rectory, which looks haunted even at noon on a sunny day. Ursula paused reverently at the foot of his walk. She seemed to be studying his empty garage.

"I wonder if he got his gum yet?" she said. "Come on. Let's peek in his mailbox."

I followed her uneasily up the walk, and we knelt by a slit in the front door. Ursula pressed her face against it.

"If I can see light, that means he's picked up his mail. I don't see any light."

"Nobody's home," I said. "Let's go."

Something dropped with a thud behind me. I spun around in time to see an orange cat, which had jumped from the open window above us, dart under the juniper bush nearby.

"I wonder what's in there," said Ursula. She pointed to the window.

"Probably the living room," I said. "If I had a chair, I could find out."

Ursula gave me a long hard look. "Listen," she said, "I'll boost you. If you stand on my shoulders, you can reach the sill."

"No, no," I whispered.

"Oh, Kate, you climb so much better than I do. Oh, please, Kate."

She sank down among the junipers and held out her hands. Friends, says Philip's mom, are more precious than gold. Furthermore, I was curious. So I put my feet on Ursula's shoulders. She stood up slowly, groaning a little.

My first glimpse of the room took in a white fur rug and a leather sofa big enough for the entire Grand Avenue baseball team to sit down in comfort.

"You're breaking my back," grunted Ursula. "Climb on the sill."

A bird sang, far off and lovely, as I pulled one knee

over the stone sill.

"What do you see?" exclaimed Ursula. "Quick!"

"I see a rug and a sofa and a—is that a piano?"

"Does he have a piano?"

"I can't see around the corner. What difference does it make if he has a piano?"

"It's very important," said Ursula. "It's—"

Suddenly we both heard it: the crunch of tires on gravel.

"He's coming!" shrieked Ursula. "Let's get out of here." She pushed off and shoved me over the sill into the room below.

Though the rug broke my fall, I felt a sharp pain in my ankle. When I picked myself up, I saw that I'd knocked over a little silver pedestal. Something brown and hairy and small was rolling away from me under the sofa.

The back door opened and closed. I heard rapid and terrible footsteps. Father Beasley walked into his living room.

He did not see me. His arms were full of packages, and he was talking loudly to himself. As I could not get out the way I got in, I thought it best to let him know he had a visitor. I opened my mouth to speak, and out came a howl.

Father Beasley let the packages sink noiselessly into the rug. Then he darted over to me and gripped me by my shoulders. He looked like a huge bat.

"Be quiet! Be quiet!" he pleaded. He loosened his grip, and I stopped crying long enough to draw a breath.

"What are you doing in my house?" he demanded, but he didn't look as mad as before.

"We—we wanted to know if you had a piano," I whispered.

He stared blankly at me for a moment, and then light dawned in his face. "Was it you who pasted Wonderbread stickers all over the altar before morning prayer yesterday?"

I shook my head. "Ursula boosted me," I said.

He let go of my shoulders and waited for details.

So I told him about the gumballs and about Ursula's stuck neck. Well, the gumballs led to the way Ursula can close her eyes and watch the movie of Father Beasley's life at any hour of the day or night, and why she needed to know what his living room looked like, as that part was always out of focus. You can't look at a room you've never seen. When I'd emptied myself of every last detail, I drew a deep breath and waited. I figured it was his turn now.

His eyes scanned the living room. "How long have you been here?" he asked.

"I just arrived."

"There was something on the pedestal," he said. "Did you take it?"

"It rolled under the sofa," I told him, eager to please. "I can reach it."

And I scooted down on my stomach and swished my arm under the sofa till my hand touched what felt like an old leather ball wearing a beard. But when I pulled it out, I discovered it was not a ball. It was a very small head.

"Wow! A shrunken head!" I yelled. "Where'd you get it?"

"A present," mused Father Beasley, "from a man whose son I baptized in the Philippines." He leaned forward and studied it, as if he, too, were hearing this information for the first time.

Oh, it was the most wonderful, fearful thing I've ever laid eyes on. A woman's face, broad-nosed, her lids stitched closed, her skin hard and dry. Her long black hair brushed my cheek as I bent over to study her. I thought I was going to be scared, but I wasn't.

Father Beasley took her from me and set her on the pedestal.

"Is she real?" I whispered.

"Absolutely," said Father Beasley. "She's worth—"

He checked himself, so I never found what she's worth. I wanted to ask if she was someone he knew. Or some saint, maybe. But he changed the subject.

"Let me make myself perfectly clear. You are never to do anything of this kind again. Do you hear me?"

"Yes," I promised and limped to the front door.

"Wait a moment. Where do you live?"

"Grand Avenue."

"I'll take you home."

There were a lot of questions I'd like to have asked him, but I couldn't bring myself to say anything except "Second house on the right" and "Thank you."

When I got home, there was a most awful smell of skunk. My ankle felt as if I'd broken it in a hundred places. I snuck into the dining room with my excuse all ready, but Mom hadn't even started dinner. She was standing with Ellen and Mrs. Fitzpatrick at the kitchen window. The window was white with steam. They'd made three peepholes in the steam and were all staring intently at the back yard. Mom was pressing an ice pack to her cheek. Papa was upstairs taking a shower and bawling out the universe.

"I don't understand it," said Mother. "I just don't."

"Tell him to scrub with tomato juice," said Mrs. Fitzpatrick.

"But Papa can't wash his gabardine suit in tomato juice," said Ellen.

I hobbled over to the window. On the hill, under the bug lights we use only in summer, dozens of skunks were converging on my rabbit trap.

"You must have the only female in the neighborhood," said Mrs. Fitzpatrick. "Imagine!"

"I just don't understand why a skunk would crawl under that box," Mom said, and she rubbed the ice pack up and down her face. Her cheek had swelled out like a pouch, the way it always does when she's just had a tooth pulled.

"How was the party for Dr. DeWigg?" I asked, hoping the guests hadn't eaten all the mints and pecans.

Mother shook her head. "We had to call it off. On account of the smell."

"It's just as well, with your mouth feeling so bad," said Mrs. Fitzpatrick.

"When Papa finishes his shower, he's taking us to McDonald's for dinner," sang Ellen.

"I think I sprained my ankle," I murmured, but nobody heard me.

"I can't go anywhere looking like this," Mom wailed. "My mouth is killing me."

We ate cold Dinty Moore's for supper, right out of the can, and Papa used the last of the Ace bandage to bind my ankle before he sent me to bed. It didn't hurt much any more. I took the telephone from the hall and hid it under the covers and called Ursula. Together we made a list of everything I could remember in Father Beasley's house.

Ellen had left a copy of *The Good Times* on my bureau, to remind me it was my turn to deliver it before school. I read it over quickly, checking for errors, but it looked perfect to me, and I was too sleepy to read it again.

The Good Times

Griselda DeWigg will celebrate her one-hundredth birthday next week.

Hildegarde Bash cut down two trees and fixed a new hook for her clothesline. She is putting a new roof on her house. Congratulations, Mrs. Bash.

Walter Bull went to the store for his mother Thursday. "That's news right there," said Mrs. Bull.

Mr. Bash got up at eleven o'clock Saturday morning.

Mrs. Bull got up at five A.M. on Tuesday to say hello to Mr. Bash. Nobody answered the door, but she received a grunt through the window. You remember in our last issue, Mr. Bash complained that no one has said hello to him for a month.

Philip Fitzpatrick fell off the cannon at the public library, wore his Frankenstein fangs to Communion, and cut his chin on a radiator valve. His cast comes off next week. Also, Walter Smith bit him on the bus.

Dr. DeWigg took her constitutional at eleven o'clock today. Her cat made it as far as the apple tree.

BELIEVE IT OR NOT:

Mrs. Sarah McMonegal of Chester, Pennsylvania, had her corn neatly removed by a hatchet falling upon it.

A catfish wearing glasses was caught by Robert Whitmore of Bristol, Virginia.

Dr. Kuji Yoshida of Tokyo, Japan, has eaten 8,280 pounds of spinach in six years in a successful attempt to grow robust and healthy.

Bono, a French dwarf who was only 18 inches tall at the age of eleven, ate 40 large cucumbers, 30 figs, and a whole watermelon for dessert each day.

WANT ADS

Wanted: one alarm clock. Mrs. Bash.

Wanted: one suitcase, used. Mr. Bash.

To be given away: 5 kitchens, 2 black and white, 2 yellow, 1 white with gray spots. Mr. & Mrs. Fitzpatrick.

Nine

THE NEXT AFTERNOON MRS. FITZ-
patrick called to complain that her phone had been
ringing all morning. I told her I was sorry about the
misprint. We aim to print nothing but the truth, I told
her.

"You'll have thin pickings in this neighborhood for
your next issue," she snorted. "Nobody cares a fig for
anything around here except tricks and foolery."

That was true. The whole neighborhood had gone
crazy over magic, except our mothers, who were the
audience. Little kids who couldn't do any real tricks ran
around with maple seeds on their noses, walnut shells on
their eyelids, and lemon peels on their teeth. The Magic
Shop was so crowded you could hardly get your toe in
the door, and Sebastian was selling tricks so fast you'd
have thought they were real magic, not the kind you
learn from a book. Mostly he sold the cheap ones, card
tricks and double-bottomed match boxes, because kids
didn't really come to buy. They came to watch Sebastian.

Oh, Sebastian, he was something to watch.

He could slice a banana without opening it, roll ten
pennies simultaneously on his knuckles, and pull paper
palm trees out of folded newspapers. He could crush a
beer can with one hand, his left one, and I happen to
know he is right-handed. He could lift his baby brother
Thomas off the floor by biting his belt and standing up
fast, with Thomas dangling from his chin like a freshly

caught mouse. Those tricks weren't for sale.

And after each sleight of hand, he'd say, "Wait till you see the Great Escapo."

The magic show was set for one o'clock on Saturday, at the public library. Mom finally agreed to let Ellen and me go if we promised not to hang around afterward. Our piano recital started promptly at three. I had hoped we could play on a stage, but Mom said it was to be held in the basement of the Methodist church.

"And that's across town from the library," said Mom as she cleared her papers from the breakfast table, "so we'll have to hurry."

Half an hour before the magic show started, the children's reading room in the public library was packed with kids. Kids on the chairs, kids on the tables, kids on the floor, and all eyes fixed on the little folding table set up next to the checkout desk. It was painted with moons and stars. You knew at a glance it belonged to the magician. Mrs. Lopez, the librarian, opened the windows. The air was so warm it felt like summer instead of the middle of October.

Ellen and I wiggled ourselves to a place on the floor, between Frances and Olivia. I stole a quick glance around me. Walter, Philip, Tony, Ursula in her jodhpurs, even though she doesn't ride any more—the whole gang was there. Sebastian slouched against the checkout desk, petting his new moustache.

"You sure are dressed up for going to the library," said Olivia, fingering the ruffle on the bottom of my pinafore.

I shrugged. "Ellen and I have a piano recital after the show."

Mrs. Lopez closed the door and clapped her hands. "The Great Escapo cannot begin his show until it's perfectly quiet," she shouted.

Everybody stopped talking at once. In that instant, the Great Escapo appeared.

He was a feast for the eyes, as my mother says of sights not easily forgotten. His suit was bright gold; you could have read a book by the light it gave off. He sleeked his silver hair behind his ears and bowed to our applause. Then he beamed his broad smile at us and inquired, "Does anybody in this room want a dog?"

A forest of hands shot up, including mine. The Great Escapo scanned our faces rapidly. Then he pointed his silver wand at a little girl with long black curls in the front row. I nearly died of envy.

"Step up here beside me," said the magician. "What's your name?"

"Sally," she whispered, stumbling forward.

"All right, Sally," said the magician. "Have you ever used a magic wand before? No?" He turned to the rest of us and let us know, with a flourish of his hand, that the success of his art rested on our attention. "Let's give Sally this wand to use."

He put the small black stick in her hand. It looked like a bald paintbrush. No good can come from that, I thought, and I sat forward to be sure nothing happened that I didn't know about.

"Now I take a perfectly ordinary balloon—"

He held up a perfectly ordinary balloon. Blue. My

favorite color.

"—and I blow it up."

He blew it up into the biggest sausage that ever was.

"Now, Sally, you wave the wand while I blow a little magic dust on the balloon."

Whether it was the dust or the wand I don't know, but this is the honest truth: the balloon started turning into a dog. The Great Escapo pinched it here and there, and soon we saw the back legs and then we saw the front, and all the while the Great Escapo was chattering away about how this was no ordinary dog, which nobody needed to be told, because who ever heard of a blue dog?

"A twist of the nose and—it's a poodle! All my poodles are pedigreed and have papers to go with 'em."

As applause broke like thunder, he handed the little girl a balloon and an old newspaper. I didn't laugh. I didn't clap. I wanted a real dog, not a balloon that went on being a balloon in spite of all he had done to it. Olivia clapped hard and leaned across me and called to Frances, "Isn't that wonderful?"

You could see Frances was only clapping to be polite. "The magician who pulled me out of a hat when I was two weeks old was ten times better than this one," she said.

But the magician was bowing right, left, and center. "See, Sally is magic, too," he smiled. "Let's give her a real nice hand."

The little girl turned red and sat down clutching

her balloon. She smiled gratefully up at the magician, but he had his mind on bigger and better tricks.

"Boys and girls, you know magicians always pull rabbits out of hats, don't they? I'm sorry to say that my hat ran out of magic and my rabbit ran away. So I brought you a little snack instead. A delicious chocolate cake, which I baked in my own magic kitchen."

From under the table he drew a cake platter, discreetly covered. When he lifted the cover, a general groan went up. The plate was empty. The Great Escapo scratched his head and frowned.

"Now, isn't that disappointing? My magic rabbit must have stolen the cake. Do you think my magic rabbit stole the cake?"

Half the kids shouted yes, the other half shouted no. It did not seem a satisfactory way of settling the question. The Great Escapo realized this also.

"Let's ask my magic rabbit to return it. I hope he didn't eat it. I'll put the cover back on the plate, and now before your very eyes—well, they don't have to be *very* eyes, they can be *blue* eyes or *brown* eyes—"

Chattering pleasantly, he waved his wand over the cover. Then very slowly he lifted it. The room grew so still you could have heard a flea breathing. Something limp and most unrabbitlike had arrived on the plate. The Great Escapo picked it up and shook it out, and held up for our approval an ordinary hand puppet.

We hissed and booed. The magician looked hurt. "You don't like this rabbit?"

"We want a real one!" I shouted.

Light dawned in the magician's eyes. It wasn't a light I trusted.

"Oh, it's the wrong kind of rabbit, is it? Well, let me try again. Whenever I do my rabbit trick, this fellow gets in the way."

He arranged the false rabbit on the plate, popped on the cover, and waved his wand. Once. Twice. The air hummed with magic. Three times, then he raised the cover.

Everybody gasped.

There on the cake platter huddled the most beautiful white rabbit I have ever seen. How can I tell you? He had pink eyes, and his ears were thinner than pea pods and pink as the inside of a sea shell. I wanted to lay my cheek against his fur.

But the magician only lifted the rabbit from the plate and tucked him into a little hutch under the table. Just as if he were an ordinary rabbit. Before we could ask him about the chocolate cake, Sebastian sidled forward wheeling a big box. It had a frame stuck on top. Across the middle of the frame glittered a knife.

"You've heard of the guillotine," he said.

A few kids snickered.

"For those of you who don't know how the guillotine works, let me demonstrate with this carrot."

He took a carrot from his pocket and held it under the blade.

He pulled the string.

Snap! Down dropped the blade, and the top of the carrot bounced across the floor. Olivia seized it and jammed it into her pocket.

"Boys and girls, I am going to drop this blade on a human neck. It will pass through the neck of the victim, and the victim will walk away without a scratch. But in order to do this remarkable trick, I need a volunteer."

Silence.

"No volunteers? I have a special whistle for the boy or girl who volunteers. It makes a sound only dogs can hear."

From another pocket he plucked a silver whistle threaded on a chain of gold. "When you blow this whistle, every dog in your neighborhood will come running."

A hundred pairs of eyes regarded the whistle.

"What if they don't?" said Philip.

"They always come," answered the Great Escapo.

Suddenly I saw myself enjoying a life of leisure. No more traps, and all the dogs I could feed. I saw my new watch gleaming on my wrist, courtesy of the Rotary Club. I raised my hand.

"Oh, Kate!" cried Ursula.

The magician smiled at me. "We have a volunteer. Step right up, young lady, and tell us your name."

"Kate," I squeaked.

"KATE," thundered the magician. "All right, let's have a big hand for the bravest girl at the show." A feeble applause rippled through the room. I saw row on row of kids too scared to clap.

"Now, Kate," said the magician, "feel this blade very carefully."

I touched it with my fingertips and drew back fast.

My mother never leaves knives that sharp loose in our kitchen.

"It's very sharp, isn't it?" observed the Great Escapo.

I bowed my head. My skin prickled into goose bumps, my bones turned to ice, and the rest of me had to pee.

"All right, Kate, I want you to stick your head through the frame and rest your chin on this strip of felt. I'm going to lock your head in place with this little door, to hold it steady."

A black door swung out of nowhere and held me fast. Reaching behind my ear, the Great Escapo brought out a golden key and fitted it into the lock. I knew I had no key behind my ear when I walked into the room, and I wondered how long it had lain there and how it knew I would raise my hand.

The lock gave a loud click. It was brass and big as a dinner plate and had a mean look. The audience observed a respectful silence while the Great Escapo twitched the string that held my life in the balance, between his thumb and pointer.

I wanted to weep. What if I died? That was a terrible way to die, in the public library, in a guillotine. But perhaps nobody else had ever died as I would, and now at the close of my life I would get into the *Guinness Book of World Records*. Too bad I couldn't live to enjoy it. Probably I would be dead very soon.

On the other hand, probably I wouldn't. Kind Mrs. Lopez wouldn't pay a magician to murder people in the children's reading room.

"Ready? Pull!" shouted the Great Escapo.

The blade dropped. It made a huge clang on the way down, and all the hairs on my neck stood up for a better view. Before they had time to lie down again, everyone was clapping.

"Let's give Kate a big hand, shall we? This girl has nerves of steel."

He bent down to unhook the little door. I basked in the roar of applause. The Great Escapo fitted the golden key into the lock and fiddled with it for a few minutes. The clapping died down. The Great Escapo signaled to Mrs. Lopez. "A little trouble with the key," he murmured.

Mrs. Lopez applied her nail file to the lock and rattled it significantly. Nothing happened. She handed the nail file to the magician. He tried it and handed it to her. Mrs. Lopez yanked a hairpin out of her head and handed it to him. Pretty soon they were passing instruments back and forth like a couple of surgeons.

"Try the wand!" called Olivia.

The Great Escapo smiled. Sweat glittered over his upper lip.

"What we really need," he announced, "is a good pair of pliers."

"I'll call the janitor," said Mrs. Lopez. "Kate, does your neck hurt?"

"No, but my back does."

"Bring her a chair," said the Great Escapo. "I have to finish my show. Kate, Mrs. Lopez will bring you a chair, and you can watch the rest of the show from the guillotine. I'll bet you've never watched a magic show from a guillotine before, have you?"

"No," I said.

He did a couple of card tricks involving the ace of hearts, and then some fancy work with scarves and ropes, but nobody paid him much attention. Mostly they were watching me. Mrs. Petrie, the janitor, appeared waving a mallet and pliers. Ellen stood by me, looking out for my interests. The magician folded his table. Parents were beginning to arrive. Mom came running up to me. "Hurry," she said. "Your recital is starting in five minutes."

"She can't go," said Ellen.

"I can't go," I said.

"What do you mean you can't go?"

"She's stuck," said Ellen.

The Great Escapo made a path through the parents who were flocking around me, wondering what I'd done.

"A little difficulty with the apparatus," explained the magician. "It's never given me trouble before. Never."

Mrs. Petrie waved a saw.

"The lock is jammed," she said. "If you want to get her out, you got to break the door down."

"Don't break the door!" cried the magician. "Do you know how much this apparatus costs new?"

"I have to go to the bathroom," I said.

"We're going to be la-a-a-ate," sang Ellen. "We're going to be la-a-a-ate!"

My mother gave the Great Escapo her whammy look. "We'll be back," she said.

While Mrs. Petrie banged on the lock with her mallet, I thought about Ellen. I saw her settling herself on the piano bench, hands rounded over the keyboard. Now she was launching into the opening bars of our duet. It would sound funny with just the bass: *oom pah pah.*

"Hey, Kate!"

There stood Mr. Goldberg, his arms full of books. "Does the librarian also set traps?" he inquired.

I told him the truth. I told him that if I ever got out of the guillotine, I would only have to blow my magic whistle, and all the dogs on earth would obey me. Mr. Goldberg listened gravely.

"Okay, let's try it," he said. "Give me the whistle."

"I don't have the whistle," I said.

Mr. Goldberg turned to the Great Escapo. "Magician, you should be ashamed of yourself. You didn't even give her the whistle."

When I had the whistle in my hand, I raised it to my lips and blew good and loud. Mrs. Lopez covered her ears. I waited for poodles, setters, terriers, Great Danes, whatever the world could offer me, to charge through the open door of the public library.

Nothing happened.

"You better give her something real, magician," said Mr. Goldberg.

"How about a blue dog?" suggested the Great Escapo, ransacking his pockets for a balloon.

"I don't want a blue dog," I wailed. "I want a white rabbit. A real one."

The Great Escapo paled. Mr. Goldberg seemed not to notice.

"I'm good at picking locks, Kate," he said. "I used to be a burglar. Murph the Second-story Artist, they called me. Do you believe me, Kate?"

"No!" I howled.

"Well, you're a pretty sharp girl, because that time I was fibbing."

He struck the head of his cane sharply against the lock. The door gave a groan and sprang open.

"Don't forget your rabbit," he added.

Into my arms the Great Escapo nestled the rabbit. Soft, warm, and mine.

"Have you a ride?" asked Mrs. Lopez.

"Kate is walking me home," said Mr. Goldberg. "It's only ten blocks."

"Ten blocks!" exclaimed the magician. "She can't carry a rabbit in her arms for ten blocks."

"Of course she can," said Mr. Goldberg.

I couldn't speak for joy. At that moment I could have carried a dozen rabbits all the way to China.

Ten

THE MAGIC CRAZE DISAPPEARED
like a puff of smoke, and with the pet show only a week
away, everybody wanted animals. There was a rush on
fleas, which our *Weekly Reader* at school informed us
could be trained to perform remarkable tricks. Walter
made two dollars selling fleas off his old cat, who is too
fat to learn any new tricks and can't remember any old
ones.

The Little Escapo was without fleas or faults. He
lived in my bedroom. Morning and evening I fed him
rabbit pellets and lettuce and considered my competition. Frances would enter her goldfish, Tony his parakeet. Olivia got two caterpillars from the science
teacher, but the day after she brought them home they
retired into their cocoons, and I knew they wouldn't
make much of a show. Ursula wrote her dad and asked
him to send her horse, although horses are not normally
allowed in our school gym. He didn't. He sent a picture
of it instead. We finally decided she could enter the
picture if she brought a note from home saying it really
was her horse and only its great size prevented it from
joining us on this happy occasion.

Nobody else I knew of had a rabbit. Since the
weather remained warm, Mom made him a hutch
outside, under the spirea bushes. After school, kids
stopped by to gaze at him. Every time you looked out
the window, you'd see half a dozen people gathered
around the hutch. In the morning my mother set up

folding chairs in front of it, and in the evening she took them away again.

"For the spectators," she said.

Papa fixed a lock on the door of the hutch. "With a name like Escapo—" he said, and he called to our minds the great Houdini, mighty magician, master of all cages but the one that killed him. I shuddered.

At night we'd bring the Little Escapo into the living room and set his box in front of the TV for the six o'clock news. He'd turn his profile to the screen and watch with his left eye for a while, then he'd hunch round the other way and give his right eye a look. Oh, he was smart, that rabbit.

"You have Mr. Goldberg to thank for that rabbit," said Mom. "Didn't he tell you once he used to practice law? I wonder how he got so good at picking locks."

She gave me a loaf of fresh pumpkin bread to take to him and naturally he offered me a piece. I sat on his baggy old sofa and ate three slices.

"Did you really used to burgle things?" I asked.

Mr. Goldberg laughed.

"I only burgled one thing in my life."

"An alligator?"

"A prayer shawl. It happened on Yom Kippur. I was poor, without prospects, far from my family, and in love with Rachel. I sat downstairs in the synagogue, among the wanderers and students. Rachel sat upstairs with her mother. Halfway through the service, the boy next to me passed me a note, carefully taped shut. I opened it and recognized Rachel's writing. The note said 'I love you.' After the service I rushed out in a daze, still clutching the prayer shawl around me. The crowds were huge, nobody noticed. I ran all the way home before I discovered it myself."

"Do you still have the prayer shawl?"

"No, I mailed it back to the synagogue. I was studying law so I could be a judge, and I didn't want the rabbi to think I stole it."

I knew right then that Mr. Goldberg had at least nine lives, like a cat.

"What does a judge do?" I asked.

"He listens to both sides and tries to hit on the truth."

"Like an umpire?" I asked.

"Like an umpire," said Mr. Goldberg. "The more hidden the truth, the higher the hit."

"Only you have to be a judge to get that kind of hit," I said.

"No, you don't," said Mr. Goldberg. "A hit is a triumph of right over wrong, joy over grief, weak over strong. We're all in this same game together, Kate."

"What was your highest hit?" I asked.

He thought for a moment. "The Great Escapo," said Mr. Goldberg, and we both laughed.

The day before the pet show, Ursula's dad sold her horse out from under her. Friends are better than silver or gold, says Philip's mom. So I agreed to let Ursula share the Great Escapo. If we won the watch, she could wear it on Monday, Wednesday, and Friday, and I could wear it on Tuesday, Thursday, and Saturday. On Sunday, we'd take turns. I'd wear it every other Sunday, which seemed fair enough.

That afternoon I took Escapo to Mrs. Quinn's beauty parlor for a dry shampoo, guaranteed, said Ursula, to give sheen and body to the most unmanageable hair. A dozen ladies peered out from under the dryers at Escapo. He sat on my lap while Ursula poured on the powder and combed it through his fur. Mrs. Quinn was putting pincurls on Mrs. Fitzpatrick's head, snipping off the strands that wanted to go their own way.

Suddenly Thomas toddled into the room, his diaper half off. Tony was supposed to be minding him, but Mrs. Quinn whacked his bare bottom and scolded Thomas instead of Tony.

"Thomas, honey, you *know* you're supposed to use the toilet. Do you think I *like* having a horse on the toilet seat?"

"All done," said Ursula, and she stood back to admire our rabbit. He was white, smooth, and bright-eyed.

"Bring him into my room, Kate," said Ursula, "and I'll put one of my hair ribbons on him. The finishing touch."

I didn't feel like walking home, so I called Papa for a ride. All the way home my stomach hurt. I felt hot, then cold, then terrible.

"Papa," I said, "I'm carsick."

"It's all in your head," said Papa.

Which I already knew, because I could feel it rolling around in there. By the time we got home, I couldn't even think about food. Papa watched me put Escapo in his hutch for the night.

"Won't be many more nights warm enough to leave him outside," said Papa.

Though I announced I was sick, nobody took much notice of it. Ellen went right on setting the table, and Mom stayed slouched over the kitchen counter, paying close attention to the school lunch menu.

"Tomorrow you're having baked beans and canned pears," she informed me. "You can buy your lunch tomorrow."

"I hate pears," I said.

"Me, too," said Ellen.

Mom looked hurt. "You should learn to like them. There's nothing offensive about pears."

"Nobody in the whole school likes pears, Mother," I said.

"Oh, I get so tired of packing lunches," moaned Mom.

Suddenly, to my great surprise, I threw up in the sink. Mom slid off the stool fast, and the menu glided to the floor.

"Go to bed," said Mom, and she hustled me upstairs.

While I was putting on my pajamas, I heard her calling Trudy on the downstairs phone, and I picked up the extension to find out how sick I was.

"Can you come in tomorrow morning?" said Mom's voice. "I've got some stuff to look up in the library before my class. Kate has an upset stomach."

"There's something—going—around," rasped Trudy

in ominous tones, as if my upset stomach was the ringleader in a vast conspiracy. "It's all laid out in the Bible. In the last days there shall be sickness and gnashing of teeth. Oh, the sun shall turn black and the moon shall become as blood, and the stars of heaven shall fall, for the Lord's wrath is great, and on the last day, who shall be able to stand?"

"Do you think," said Mom, "you could just come tomorrow morning at eight?"

The pet show wouldn't start, I thought, until three in the afternoon. By afternoon I might be well enough to make a brief appearance. Last winter I had a fever of a hundred and four the night of the Ice Follies, and Mom let me skate with my class anyhow because I'd practiced the routine every day for six weeks. When I heard Trudy hang up, I put down the receiver and called, "Mom, can I still go to the pet show?"

"We'll see," said Mom.

"Do I have to go to school?"

"No."

Since I didn't have to go to school, I took my time going to bed. I brushed my teeth. I brushed my tongue. I put my statue of Babe Ruth on the bureau. It's white, like Ivory soap, and Babe Ruth is smiling and stretching out his hand to catch the ball. I stood at the top of the stairs and called, "Can I sleep on the sofa?" I love waking up in strange places.

"No," Mother called back. "You're sick. Go to bed, and I'll come upstairs to check your temperature."

I crawled under the eiderdown and observed that the wisteria vine outside my window had caught a star. I made a quick wish on it, about a wrist watch. The last thing I saw before I fell asleep was Babe Ruth's smile and his raised hand, small and white in the moonlight, blessing me.

THE NEXT MORNING I LISTENED for the clatter of pans in the kitchen. Silence. That meant it was still early. The front door slammed: Ellen was going out to feed Escapo for me. I jumped out of bed, rummaged through my closet, and found my shopping bag of treats from last Halloween. There were five candy corns left. I ate them slowly and happily. In another week, it would be time to replenish my hoard.

Suddenly Ellen rushed into the room. "He's gone!" she gasped.

"Who's gone?"

"Escapo. He's not in his cage. Oh, Kate, what's wrong with you? You look so funny!"

I couldn't believe I'd forgotten to lock the hutch. A thousand possibilities raced through my mind. Maybe he hadn't been gone long. Maybe he would see me drooping by the empty hutch and come back. I ran to the door of my room and collided with Mom, holding an empty aspirin bottle in one hand and her head in the other.

"We're clean out," she said. "And I've got such a headache. I'll pick up another—my God, you're all spots!" She threw the bottle on my dresser. "Ellen, get out at once."

Ellen backed away like a crab.

"What's wrong with me?" I cried.

Mother started running around, pulling down the shades. "It might be measles," she said. Then, seeing my scared face, she added, "Of course, it might not be. There are two kinds of measles. The long kind and the short kind."

"What kind do I have?"

"I don't know."

By the time Trudy arrived, she had decided it was the short kind, as I hadn't much fever. I lay in bed, listening to the eight o'clock rush below me. I told myself that Escapo was tame. He loved me. He would return.

Then Ellen left for school. Mom and Dad left for work, Trudy retired to the kitchen, and silence settled over the house. I thought of Escapo, his white fur, his tender ears, the wrist watch he might have won me, and I started to cry. Trudy marched upstairs, mumbling.

"You think you got troubles," she snorted. "Harold is out on parole, and he's around the house all day. Can't get a job nohow."

She sat down in my little rocking chair, pulled a handkerchief out of her blouse, and blew her nose. "When a man goes out to work, he don't come back till late and you got the whole day to relax and listen to the radio and sew. Now I got to worry about him, hanging around all day and staying out all night. He'll run Saturday and Sunday and conk out Monday morning. Saturday and Sunday are my worst days."

Today was Friday. I doubted my troubles would impress her much.

"I just can't take an interest in barroom life," she said in a choked voice. "I haven't gone drinking since the day I married him. I settled down. I let my hair grow straight, took my jewelry off, started going to church. Oh, the Devil works hard in a person trying to do right."

The full weight of her grief broke over our heads, and we both started to sob.

"All I do is go to church, work, and pay my bills," she wailed. "What kind of life is that for a young lady of promise and ambition? I got to make myself independent."

I leaped out of bed and threw my arms around her. "Oh, Trudy, if I win the pet show, I'll give you my watch to sell."

As I swore this vow, I remembered I had no pet. I also remembered the wishing star in the wisteria vine. I felt cheated. Stars have always done right by me before.

"Trudy, if I wish on a star, will I get my wish?"

"No," said Trudy, sniffling.

"Who gets it, then?"

Trudy didn't answer, just wiped her nose on the back of her hand. I thought of the watch I wouldn't win. The more I tried to put it out of my mind, the more it took root there. By the time my parents would buy me a watch, I would be too old to enjoy it. A huge sob rose in my throat. I swallowed it noisily.

"I suppose you want some jello," said Trudy, rising. "That's good for sick stomachs. Go back to bed."

I didn't want her to go and leave me with no one to talk to. "Trudy," I said, "have you had measles?"

"Lord, yes! I wouldn't be standing here if I hadn't."

Later, she brought up the jello on a tray, along with

the radio and her crocheting. The radio, we discovered, was dead. The jello was lively and wiggled right off the spoon.

"Don't make a mess," said Trudy. She pulled up the shades a tiny bit, so she could see her hook and thread.

"Trudy," I said, "why do people get sick?"

"Germs," answered Trudy.

"What are germs?" I asked.

"Germs are very small animals."

I was at once interested. "How small?"

"Smaller than dust. Smaller than those motes you see in a ray of sunlight."

"Could I catch one?"

"Lord, yes. You caught one already. This room is full of germs."

"How do I catch one?"

Trudy sighed. Then she waved her arm, closed her fist, and opened it cautiously over the empty aspirin bottle and clapped the cap on. "There," she said.

"Did you catch one?" I asked.

"Thousands," Trudy assured me. And she tossed the bottle into the wastebasket.

"Don't!" I exclaimed, snatching it. "I need that bottle."

Trudy got up and went away shaking her head.

I had a plan. I had such a good plan that I stopped worrying about Escapo and pulled out my box of baseball cards from under my bed and spent the day sorting them according to team, year, and oddness of name. If I kept my traps baited, Escapo would return.

In the meantime, I had my plan. I fell asleep and woke up under a light blanket of baseball cards. Somebody was banging at the window.

I jumped up in alarm. On the roof hunkered Ursula, horsey and sorrowful in her jodhpurs and riding boots, her face pressed to the glass.

"You really look funny," she shouted.

"So do you," I shouted back.

"Is it true you lost Escapo?"

I nodded and drew myself up to the window and tugged at the lock. "But I have another pet, and this one's sure to win."

And I waved the aspirin bottle. Ursula stretched out her hand. I cracked the window open and sent my plan out into the world. Ursula put her eye to the bottle as if it were a telescope.

"I can't see anything," she said. "What's in there?"

"Charlie, the remarkable germ," I said. "He'll win first prize for the smallest pet."

"Pet?" Ursula looked doubtful.

"Germs are *real* animals, Ursula. Everybody knows that."

"But Kate, he's got to win in two categories, or we won't get the watch."

I was feeling so good that nothing seemed impossible. "You can also enter him as the smartest pet," I added.

"What's so smart about a germ?" Ursula asked.

"He must be smart," I told her. "I'm a million times bigger than he is, and look what he did to me."

She peeped into the bottle again. "Kate, do you

think the judges will believe he's in there?"

"You'll just have to convince them," I said.

Then Ursula pocketed Charlie and dropped behind the horizon of my window. I crawled back under the covers and sent my mind over to the school gym. I saw Tony whipping his parakeet, who would be dancing for her life, and Walter lugging his cat, who would be too lazy to walk, and Frances carrying her goldfish and reminding everyone how the king of Saudi Arabia gave her a pet dolphin when she was six weeks old, which she lost the day before she was adopted. I saw Olivia opening her lunchbox before the judges to reveal a pair of cocoons, sleeping away this golden opportunity. There would be other kids, and other pets, but none smaller than mine.

An hour after I'd sent Ursula on her way, the phone rang. I bounded into my dad's study and grabbed the phone off the hook. It was Ellen.

"Kate! You won the watch!"

"I did? I did?"

"You won a ribbon for the smallest pet and a ribbon for the most original pet. Ursula is on her way over with the watch."

"But they don't have a class for the most original," I said.

"They do now. Also for the most surprising pet. Walter won that."

"What's so surprising about Walter's old cat?" I asked.

"She had kittens."

Half an hour later I heard the clatter of Ursula's

riding boots on the roof. She was waving her arms and dancing like a madwoman. "We won! We won! Open your window!"

Through the crack she pushed a wrist watch with a red plastic band, stapled to a card. On the dial smiled Mickey Mouse, crossing his arms like a referee.

"Oh, Kate, you should've been there!"

"Tell me everything," I said. "I want to know everything."

So she told me how at first the judges didn't want to give Charlie the prize, but they couldn't find anything in their rules that ruled out invisible pets. They also had to admit he was certainly the smallest pet. And in the whole history of the pet show, nobody had ever entered a germ, so he was certainly the most original pet.

"They were just getting ready to hand me the watch when a man from the Rotary Club came up and said one of the contestants wanted to register a complaint."

"Who was it?"

Ursula hesitated. "It was Tony. Tony said if you couldn't see a thing, you couldn't be sure it was there. And then Father Flannagan stood up and said he was ashamed to hear Tony, of all people, speak out against the faith, and he scolded him right in front of everybody for cutting catechism class the last two Saturdays. Tony withdrew the complaint. And we won!"

If there hadn't been a window between us, I'd have hugged Ursula.

"You can wear the watch till you get well. Did you

ever see anything so elegant?"

I took the watch off the card and wound it. Then I held it up to my ear. It didn't tick. After Ursula was gone, I tried shaking it. Nothing happened. Mom came in with my supper on a tray.

"Congratulations," she said.

"Mom," I said, "is this a real watch?"

Mother turned it over in her hand. "I think it's a toy," she said.

I was so disappointed I started to weep.

"You've been wanting a watch," said Mom. "What on earth is wrong with you?"

"I wanted a *real* watch. This one's a fake. I'm giving it back."

"You can't give it back. You won it. It's yours."

"Only half of it's mine. The other half belongs to Ursula. I'll give her my half, too. She thinks it's so elegant."

Mother took the watch downstairs. I figured I was fated never to have a watch of my own. Or maybe I would almost have one and then lose it, over and over, for the rest of my life.

But the star I wished on was smarter than I was. The next morning I woke up to find Mr. Goldberg's watch and cane lying at the foot of my bed. Before I could lay a hand on them, Mom walked in, bearing an armload of clean laundry.

"Mr. Goldberg's sister from Florida brought those over for you."

I picked them up. First the watch, then the cane,

not daring to believe they were mine. "Doesn't he want them?"

Mom turned her back on me and started folding the clean clothes into drawers. "Guess not. He's moving to Florida."

"Why is he moving to Florida?" I demanded.

"He got up to use the bathroom last night and blacked out," said Mom. "He lost consciousness. When he woke up he found himself lying at the foot of the stairs. He'd fallen down the whole flight, and he didn't remember a thing about it."

"Was he hurt?" I asked.

Mom didn't answer right away. "He didn't break any bones. Next time he might not be so lucky. He's nearly seventy-six, and he can't live alone any more. I have his sister's address. You be sure to write him a thank-you note for the watch."

Suddenly I didn't want the watch. I wanted Mr. Goldberg back again so I could tell him how I'd scored the highest hit. Weak over strong, joy over grief, and all the rest of it. What would Mr. Goldberg say if I'd left him like that, without even saying good-bye?

I knew what he'd say—"Wonderful, wonderful. We lose sight of each other, but not forever. Who can tell on what road we'll meet again?"

I turned the watch face down, the way Mr. Goldberg used to wear it, and put it on the table by my bed.

"The watch is nice, but I like the cane better," I said.

Mom laughed. "You won't be using the cane, I hope, at your age."

"I will so use it."

"For what?" asked Mom.

I jumped out of bed and showed her the first two steps of "The Taxicab."

"For dancing," I answered.